SATORI IN PARIS ANd PIC

OTHER WORKS BY JACK KEROUAC

Published by Grove Press

Dr. Sax

Lonesome Traveler

Mexico City Blues

The Subterraneans

SATORI IN PARIS
AND
PIC

TWO NOVELS BY

JACK KEROUAC

Grove Press
New York

Satori in Paris *was originally published in three installments in*
Evergreen Review
Printed in the United States of America

Library of Congress Cataloging-in-Publication Data

Kerouac, Jack, 1922–1969.
    Satori in Paris; and, Pic.
      I. Kerouac, Jack, 1922–1969. Pic. 1987.
  II. Title.   II. Title: Satori in Paris.   IV. Title:
Pic.
PS3521.E735A6   1988   813'.54   87-27948
ISBN 0-8021-3061-5

Grove Press
841 Broadway
New York, NY 10003

04 05 06 07 08   20 19 18 17 16 15 14

SATORI IN PARIS

1.

SOMEWHERE DURING MY TEN DAYS IN PARIS (AND Brittany) I received an illumination of some kind that seems to've changed me again, towards what I suppose'll be my pattern for another seven years or more: in effect, a *satori:* the Japanese word for "sudden illumination," "sudden awakening" or simply "kick in the eye."—Whatever, something *did* happen and in my first reveries after the trip and I'm back home regrouping all the confused rich events of those ten days, it seems the satori was handed to me by a taxi driver named Raymond Baillet, other times I think it might've been my paranoiac fear in the foggy streets of Brest Brittany at 3 A.M., other times I think it was Monsieur Casteljaloux and his dazzlingly beautiful secretary (a Bretonne with blue-black hair, green eyes, separated front teeth just right in eatable lips, white wool knit sweater, with

gold bracelets and perfume) or the waiter who
told me *"Paris est pourri"* (Paris is rotten) or the
performance of Mozart's Requiem in old church
of St. Germain des Prés with elated violinists
swinging their elbows with joy because so many
distinguished people had shown up crowding the
pews and special chairs (and outside it's misting)
or, in Heaven's name, *what?* The straight tree
lanes of Tuileries Gardens? Or the roaring sway
of the bridge over the booming holiday Seine
which I crossed holding on to my hat knowing it
was not the bridge (the makeshift one at Quai des
Tuileries) but I myself swaying from too much
cognac and nerves and no sleep and jet airliner
all the way from Florida twelve hours with airport
anxieties, or bars, or anguishes, intervening?

As in an earlier autobiographical book I'll use
my real name here, full name in this case, Jean-
Louis Lebris de Kérouac, because this story is
about my search for this name in France, and I'm
not afraid of giving the real name of Raymond
Baillet to public scrutiny because all I have to say
about him, in connection with the fact he may be
the cause of my satori in Paris, is that he was
polite, kind, efficient, hip, aloof and many other
things and mainly just a cabdriver who happened
to drive me to Orly airfield on my way back home
from France: and sure he wont be in trouble because of that—And besides probably never will
see his name in print because there are so many
books being published these days in America and
in France nobody has time to keep up with all of
them, and if told by someone that his name ap-
pears in an American "novel" he'll probably never

find out where to buy it in Paris, if it's ever translated at all, and if he does find it, it wont hurt him to read that he, Raymond Baillet, is a great gentleman and cabdriver who happened to impress an American during a fare ride to the airport.

Compris?

2.

BUT AS I SAY I DONT KNOW HOW I GOT THAT SATORI and the only thing to do is start at the beginning and maybe I'll find out right at the pivot of the story and go rejoicing to the end of it, the tale that's told for no other reason but companionship, which is another (and my favorite) definition of literature, the tale that's told for companionship and to teach something religious, of religious reverence, about real life, in this real world which literature should (and here does) reflect.

In other words, and after this I'll shut up, made-up stories and romances about what would happen IF are for children and adult cretins who are afraid to read themselves in a book just as they might be afraid to look in the mirror when they're sick or injured or hungover or *insane.*

3.

THIS BOOK'LL SAY, IN EFFECT, HAVE PITY ON US all, and dont get mad at me for writing at all.

I live in Florida. Arriving over Paris suburbs in the big Air France jetliner I noticed how green the northern countryside is in the summer, because of winter snows that have melted right into that butterslug meadow. Greener than any palmetto country could ever be, and especially in June before August (Août) has withered it all away. The plane touched down without a Georgia hitch. Here I'm referring to that planeload of prominent respectable Atlantans who were all loaded with gifts around 1962 and heading back to Atlanta when the liner shot itself into a farm and everybody died, it never left the ground and half of Atlanta was depleted and all the gifts were strewn and burned all over Orly, a great Christian tragedy not the fault of the French government at all since the pilots and steward's crew were all French citizens.

The plane touched down just right and here we were in Paris on a gray cold morning in June.

In the airport bus an American expatriate was calmly and joyfully smoking his pipe and talking to his buddy just arrived on another plane probably from Madrid or something. In my own plane I had not talked to the tired American painter girl because she fell asleep over Nova Scotia in the lonesome cold after the exhaustion of New York City and having to buy a million drinks for the people who were babysitting there for her— no business of mine anyhow. She'd wondered at Idlewild if I was going to look up my old flame in Paris:– no. (I really shoulda.)

For I was the loneliest man in Paris if that's possible. It was 6 A.M. and raining and I took the airport bus into the city, to near Les Invalides, then a taxi in the rain and I asked the driver where Napoleon was entombed because I knew it was someplace around there, not that it matters, but after a period of what I thought to be surly silence he finally pointed and said "là" (there).

I was all hot to go see the Sainte Chapelle where St. Louis, King Louis IX of France, had installed a piece of the True Cross. I never even made it except ten days later zipping by in Raymond Baillet's cab and he mentioned it. I was also all hot to see St. Louis de France church on the island of St. Louis in the Seine River, because that's the name of the church of my baptism in Lowell, Massachusetts. Well I finally got there and sat

with hat in hand watching guys in red coats blow
long trumpets at the altar, to organ upstairs,
beautiful Medieval *cansòs* or cantatas to make
Handel's mouth water, and all of a sudden a
woman with kids and husband comes by and lays
twenty centimes (4¢) in my poor tortured misunderstood hat (which I was holding upsidedown
in awe), to teach them *caritas*, or loving charity,
which I accepted so's not to embarrass her teach-
erly instincts, or the kids, and my mother said
back home in Florida "Why didnt you then put
the twenty centimes in the poor box" which I forgot. It wasnt enough to wonder about and besides
the very first thing I did in Paris after I cleaned
up in my hotel room (with a big round wall in it,
welling the chimney I guess) was give a franc
(20¢) to a French woman beggar with pimples,
saying *"Un franc pour la Française"* (A franc for
the Frenchwoman) and later I gave a franc to a
man beggar in St.-Germain to whom I then yelled:
"Vieux voyou!" (Old hoodlum!) and he laughed
and said: 'What?—*Hood*-lum?" I said "Yes, you
cant fool an old French Canadian" and I wonder
today if that hurt him because what I really
wanted to say was "Guenigiou" (ragpicker) but
"voyou" came out.

Guenigiou it is.

(Ragpicker should be spelled "guenillou," but
that's not the way it comes out in 300-year-old
French which was preserved intact in Quebec and
still understood in the streets of Paris not to mention the hay barns of the North.)

Coming down the steps of that magnificent huge

church of La Madelaine was a dignified old bum
in a full brown robe and gray beard, neither a
Greek nor a Patriarch, just probably an old member of the Syriac Church; either that or a Surrealist on a larky kick? Na.

4.

FIRST THINGS FIRST.

The altar in La Madelaine is a gigantic marble sculpt of her (Mary Magdalena) as big as a city block and surrounded by angels and archangels. She holds out her hands in a gesture Michelangeloesque. The angels have huge wings dripping. The place is a whole city block long. It's a long narrow building of a church, one of the strangest. No spires, no Gothic, but I suppose Greek temple style. (Why on earth would you, or did you, expect me to go see the Eiffel Tower made of Bucky Buckmaster's steel ribs and ozone? How dull can you get riding an elevator and getting the mumps from being a quarter mile in the air? I already done that orf the Hempire State Building at night in the mist with my editor.)

The taxi took me to the hotel which was a Swiss pension I guess but the nightclerk was an Etruscan (same thing) and the maid was sore at me because I kept my door and suitcase locked. The lady who ran the hotel was not pleased when I inaugurated my first evening with a wild sexball with a woman my age (43). I cant give her real name but it's one of the oldest names in French history, aye back before Charlemagne, and he was a Pippin. (Prince of the Franks.) (Descended from Arnulf, L'Évêsque of Metz.) (Imagine having to fight Frisians, Alemanni, Bavarians *and* Moors.) (Grandson of Plectrude.) Well this old gal was the wildest lay imaginable. How can I go into such detail about toilet matters. She really made me blush at one point. I shoulda told her to stick her head in the "poizette" but of course (that's Old French for toilette) she was too delightful for words. I met her in an afterhours Montparnasse gangster bar with no gangsters around. She took me over. She also wants to marry me, naturally, as I am a great natural bed mate and nice guy. I gave her $120 for her son's education, or some new-old parochial shoes. She really done my budget in. I still had enough money the next day to go on and buy William Makepeace Thackeray's *Livres des Snobs* at Gare St.-Lazare. It isnt a question of money but of souls having a good time. In the old church of St.-Germain-des-Prés that following afternoon I saw several Parisian Frenchwomen practically weeping as they prayed under an old bloodstained and rainroiled wall. I said "Ah ha, *les femmes de Paris*" and I saw the greatness of Paris that it can weep for the follies of the Revolution and at the same time rejoice they got rid of all those long nosed nobles, of which I am a descendant (Princes of Brittany).

5.

CHATEAUBRIAND WAS AN AMAZING WRITER WHO
wanted early old love affairs on a higher order
than the Order was giving him in 1790 France—
he wanted something out of a Medieval vignette,
some young gal come down the street and look him
right in the eye, with ribbons and a grandmother
sewing, and that night the house burns down. Me
and my Pippin had our healthy get-together at
some point or other in my very calm drunkenness
and I was satisfied, but next day I didnt wanta see
her no mo because she wanted *more* money. Said
she was going to take me out on the town. I told
her she owed me several more jobs, bouts, jots
and tittles.

   "Mais oui."
But I let the Etruscan fluff her off on the phone.
   The Etruscan was a pederast. In which I have
no interest, but $120 is going too far. The Etrus-
can said he was a Mountain Italian. I dont care

or know if he's a pederast or not, actually, and shouldna said that, but he was a nice kid. I then went out and got drunk. I was about to meet some of the prettiest women in the world but the bed business was over because now I was getting real stoned drunk.

6

IT'S HARD TO DECIDE WHAT TO TELL IN A STORY, AND
I always seem to try to prove something, comma,
about my sex. Let's forget it. It's just that sometimes I get terribly lonely, for the companionship
of a woman dingblast it.

So I spend all day in St.-Germain looking for
the perfect bar and I find it. *La Gentilhommière*
(Rue St. André des Arts, which is pointed out to
me by a gendarme)—Bar of the Gentle Lady—
And how gentle can you get with soft blonde hair
all golden sprayed and neat little figure? "O I wish
I was handsome" I say but they all assure me I'm
handsome—"Alright then I'm a dirty old drunk"
—"Anything you want to say"—

I gaze into her eyes—I give her the double
whammy blue eyes compassion shot—She falls for
it.

A teenage Arab girl from Algiers or Tunis

comes in, with a soft little hook nose. I'm going
out of my mind because meanwhile I'm exchang-
ing a hundred thousand French pleasantries and
conversations with Negro Princes from Senegal,
Breton Surrealist poets, boulevardiers in perfect
clothes, lecherous gynecologists (from Brittany),
a Greek bartender angel called Zorba, and the
owner is Jean Tassart cool and calm by his cash
register and looking vaguely depraved (tho actually a quiet family man who happens to look like
Rudy Loval my old buddy in Lowell Massachusetts
who'd had such a reputation at fourteen for his
many *amours* and had that same perfume of
smoothy looks). Not to mention Daniel Maratra
the other bartender, some weird tall Jew or Arab,
in any case a Semite, whose name sounded like the
trumpets in front of the walls of Granada: and a
gentler tender of bar you never saw.

In the bar there's a woman who is a lovely 40-
year-old redhead Spaniard *amoureuse* who takes
an actual liking to me, does worse and takes me
seriously, and actually makes a date for us to meet
alone: I get drunk and forget. Over the speaker
is coming endless American modern jazz over a
tape. To make up for forgetting to meet Valarino
(the redhead Spanish beauty) I buy her a tapes-
try on the Quai, from a young Dutch genius, ten
bucks (Dutch genius whose name in Dutch, Beere,
means "pier" in English). She announces she's
going to redecorate her room on account of it but
doesnt invite me over. What I woulda done to her
shall not be allowed in this Bible yet it woulda
been spelled L O V E.

I get so mad I go down to the whore districts.

A million Apaches with daggers are milling
around. I go in a hallway and I see three ladies
of the night. I announce with an evil English leer
"Sh'prend la belle brunette" (I take the pretty
brunette)—The brunette rubs her eyes, throat,
ears and heart and says "I aint gonna have that
no more." I stomp away and take out my Swiss
Army knife with the cross on it, because I suspect
I'm being followed by French muggers and thugs.
I cut my own finger and bleed all over the place. I
go back to my hotel room bleeding all over the
lobby. The Swiss woman by now is asking me
when I'm going to leave. I say "I'll leave as soon
as I've verified my family in the library." (And
add to myself: "What do you know about *les
Lebris de Kérouacks* and their motto of Love Suffer and Work you dumb old Bourgeois bag.")

7.

So I go to the library, la Bibliothèque Nationale, to check up on the list of the officers in Montcalm's Army 1756 Quebec, and also Louis Moréri's dictionary, and Père Anselme etc., all the information about the royal house of Brittany, and it aint even there and finally in the Mazarine Library old sweet Madame Oury the head librarian patiently explains to me that the Nazis done bombed and burned all their French papers in 1944, something which I'd forgotten in my zeal. Still I smell that there's something fishy in Brittany— Surely de Kérouack should be recorded in France if it's already recorded in the British Museum in London?—I tell her that—

You cant smoke even in the toilet in the Bibliothèque Nationale and you cant get a word in edgewise with the secretaries and there's a national pride about "scholars" all sitting there copying

outa books and they wouldnt even let John Montgomery in (John Montgomery who forgot his
sleeping bag on the climb to Matterhorn and is
America's best librarian and scholar and is English) —

Meanwhile I have to go back and see how the
gentle ladies are doing. My cabdriver is Roland
Ste. Jeanne d'Arc de la Pucelle who tells me that
all Bretons are "corpulent" like me. The ladies
are kissing me on both cheeks French style. A
Breton called Goulet is getting drunk with me,
young, 21, blue eyes, black hair, and suddenly
grabs Blondie and scares her (with the other fellows joining in), almost a rape, which me and the
other Jean, Tassart, put a stop to: "Awright!"
"*Arrète!*"—

"Cool it," I add.

She is just too beautiful for words. I said to her
"*Tu passe toutes la journée dans maudite* beauty
parlor?" (You spend all day in the damn beauty
parlor?)

"*Oui.*"

Meanwhile I go down to the famous cafes on
the boulevard and sit there watching Paris go by,
such hepcats the young men, motorcycles, visiting
firemen from Iowa.

8.

THE ARAB GIRL GOES OUT WITH ME, I INVITE HER TO see and hear a performance of Mozart's Requiem in old St.-Germain-des-Prés church, which I knew about from an earlier visit and saw the poster announcing it. It's full of people, crowded, we pay at the door and walk into surely the most *distingué* gathering in Paris that night, and as I say it's misting outside, and her soft little hook nose has under it rose lips.

I teach her Christianity.

We neck a little later and she goes home to her parents. She wants me to take her to the beach at Tunis, I'm wondering if I shall be stabbed by Arabs jealous on the Bikini beach and that week Boumedienne deposed and *dis*-posed of Ben Bella and that woulda been a fine kettle of fish, and also I didnt have the money now and I wonder why she

24

wanted that:– I've been told where to get off on
the beaches of Morocco.

I just dont know.

Methinks women love me and then they realize
I'm drunk for all the world and this makes them
realize I cant concentrate on them alone, for long,
makes them jealous, and I'm a fool in Love With
God. Yes.

Besides, lechery's not my meat and makes me
blush:– depends on the Lady. She was not my
style. The French blonde was, but too young for
me.

In times to come I'll be known as the fool who
rode outa Mongolia on a pony: Genghiz Khan, or
the Mongolian Idiot, *one*. Well I'm not an idiot,
and I like ladies, and I'm polite, but impolitic, like
Ippolit my cousin from Russia. An old hitch hiker
in San Francisco, called Joe Ihnat, announced that
mine was an ancient Russian name meaning
"Love." Kerouac. I said "Then they went to Scotland?"

"Yes, then Ireland, then Cornwall, Wales, and
Brittany, then you know the rest."

"*Roo*shian?"

"Means Love."

"You're kidding."

—Oh, and then I realized, "of course, outa Mongolia and the Khans, and before that, Eskimos of
Canada and Siberia. All goes back around the
world, not to mention Perish-the-Thought Persia."
(Aryans).

Anyhow me and the Breton Goulet went to an
evil bar where a hundred assorted Parisians were

eagerly listening to a big argument between a white man and a black man. I got outa there quick and left him to his own devices, met him back at La Gentilhommière, some fight musta spilled out, or, not, I wasnt there.

Paris is a tough town.

9.

THE FACT OF THE MATTER IS, HOW CAN YOU BE AN Aryan when you're an Eskimo or a Mongol? That old Joe Ihnat was full of little brown turds, unless he means Russia. Old Joe Tolstoy we shoulda picked up.

Why keep talking about such things? Because my grammar school teacher was Miss Dineen, who is now Sister Mary of St. James in New Mexico (James was a son of Mary, like Jude), and she wrote: "Jack and his sister Carolyn (Ti Nin) I remember well as friendly, cooperative children with unusual charm. We were told that their folks came from France, and that the name was de Kerouac. I always felt that they had the dignity and refinement of aristocracy."

I mention this to show that there can be such a thing as manners.

My manners, abominable at times, can be sweet.
As I grew older I became a drunk. Why? Because
I like ecstasy of the mind.

I'm a Wretch.

But I love love.

(Strange Chapter)

10.

NOT ONLY THAT BUT YOU CANT GET A NIGHT'S sleep in France, they're so lousy and noisy at 8 A.M. screaming over fresh bread it would make Abomination weep. Buy that. Their strong hot coffee and *croissants* and crackling French bread and Breton butter, Gad, where's my Alsatian beer?

While looking for the library, incidentally, a gendarme in the Place de la Concorde told me that Rue de Richelieu (street of the National Library) was thataway, pointing, and because he was an officer I was afraid to say *"What? . . NO!"* because I knew it was in the opposite direction somewhere—Here he is some kind of sergeant or other who certainly oughta know the streets of Paris giving an American tourist a bum steer. (Or did he believe I was a wise-guy Frenchman

29

pulling his leg? since my French *is* French)—But
no, he points in the direction of one of de Gaulle's
security buildings and sends me there maybe
thinking "That's the National Library alright, ha
ha ha" ("maybe they'll shoot down that Quebec
rat")—Who knows? Any Parisian middle-aged
gendarme oughta know where Rue de Richelieu is
—But thinking he may be right and I'd made a
mistake studying the Paris map back home I do
go in the direction he points, afraid to go any
other, and go down the upper spate of Champs-
Elysées then cut across the damp green park
and across Rue Gabriel to the back of an important government building of some kind where suddenly I see a sentry box and out of it steps a
guard with bayonet in full Republican Guard re-
galia (like Napoleon with a cockatoo hat) and he
snaps to attention and holds up his bayonet at
Present Arms but it's not for me really, it's for a
sudden black limousine full of bodyguards and
guys in black suits who receive a salute from the
other sentry men and zip on by—I stroll past the
sentry bayonet and take out my plastic Camel
cigarette container to light a butt—Immediately
two strolling gendarmes are passing me in the
opposite direction watching every move I make—
It turns out I'm only lighting a butt but how can
they tell? *plastic* and all that—And that is the
marvelous tight security around big old de Gaulle's
very palace which is a few blocks away.

I go down to the corner bar to have a cognac
alone at a cool table by the open door.

The bartender in there is very polite and tells
me exactly how to get to the library: right down

St.-Honoré then across la Place de la Concorde
and then Rue Rivoli right at the Louvre and left
on Richelieu to the Library dingblast it.

So how can an American tourist who doesnt
speak French get around at all? Let alone me?

To know the name of the street of the sentry
box itself I'd have to order a map from the C.I.A.

11.

A STRANGE SEVERE PAROCHIAL-STYLE LIBRARY, LA Bibliothèque Nationale on rue de Richelieu, with thousands of scholars and millions of books and strange assistant librarians with Zen Master brooms (really French aprons) who admire good *handwriting* more than anything in a scholar or writer—Here, you feel like an American genius who escaped the rules of Le Lycée. (French High School).

All I wanted was: *Histoire généalogique de plusieurs maisons illustres de Bretagne, enrichie des armes et blasons d'icelles . . .* etc. by Fr. Augustin Du Paz, Paris, N.Buon, 1620, Folio Lm² 23 et Rés. Lm 23.

Think I got it? Not on your—

And also I wanted:– Pêre Anselme de Sainte Marie, (*né* Pierre de Guibours), his *Histoire de la maison royale de France, des puirs, grands*

*officiers de la couronne et de la maison du roy
et des anciens barons du royaume*, R.P. Anselme,
Paris, E. Loyson 1674, Lm³ 397, (History of the
royal house of France, and of also, the great
officers of the crown and of the house of the
king and of the ancient barons of the kingdom),
all of which I had to write down neatly as I could
on the call-cards and the old aproned fella told the
old lady librarian "It's well written" (meaning the
legibility of the handwriting). Of course they all
smelled the liquor on me and thought I was a nut
but on seeing I knew what and how to ask for cer-
tain books they all went in back to huge dusty files
and shelves as high as the roof and must've drawn
up ladders high enough to make Finnegan fall
again with an even bigger noise than the one in
Finnegans Wake, this one being the noise of the
name, the actual name the Indian Buddhists gave
to the Tathagata or passer-through of the Aeon
Priyadavsana more than Incalculable Aeons ago:–
Here we go, Finn:–

GALADHARAGARGITAGHOSHASUSVARA-
NAKSHATRARAGASANKUSUMITABHIGNA.

Now I mention this to show, that if I didnt
know libraries, and specifically the greatest library in the world, the New York Public Library
where I among a thousand other things actually
copied down this long Sanskrit name exactly as
it's spelled, then why should I be regarded with
suspicion in the Paris Library? Of course I'm not
young any more and "smell of liquor" and even
talk to interesting Jewish scholars in the library
there (one Éli Flamand copying down notes for a

history of Renaissance art and who kindly as-
sisted me's much's he could), still I dont know,
it seemed they really thought I was nuts when
they saw what I asked for, which I copied from
their *incorrect* and incomplete files, not fully what
I showed you above about Père Anselme as written in the completely correct files of London, as I
found later where the national records were not
destroyed by fire, saw what I asked for, which did
not conform to the actual titles of the old books
they had in the back, and when they saw my name
Kerouac but with a "Jack" in front of it, as tho
I were a Johann Maria Philipp Frimont von Palota suddenly traveling from Staten Island to the
Vienna library and signing my name on the call-
cards Johnny Pelota and asking for Hergott's
Genealogia augustae gentis Habsburgicae (incomplete title) and my name not spelled "Palota," as
it should, just as my real name should be spelled
"Kerouack," but both old Johnny and me've been
thru so many centuries of genealogical wars and
crests and cockatoos and gules and jousts against
Fitzwilliams, agh—
It doesnt matter.
And besides it's all too long ago and worthless
unless you can find the actual family monuments
in fields, like with me I go claim the bloody dolmens of Carnac? Or I go and claim the Cornish
language which is called Kernuak? Or some little
old cliff-castle at Kenedjack in Cornwall or one of
the "hundreds" called Kerrier in Cornwall? Or
Cornouialles itself outside Quimper and Keroual?
(Brittany thar).
Well anyway I was trying to find things out

about my old family, I was the first Lebris de
Kérouack ever to go back to France in 210 years
to find out and I was planning to go to Brittany
and Cornwall England next (land of Tristan and
King Mark) and later I was gonna hit Ireland
and find Isolde and like Peter Sellers get banged
in the mug in a Dublin pub.

Ridiculous, but I was so happy on cognac I was
going to try.

The whole library groaned with the accumu-
lated debris of centuries of recorded folly, as tho
you had to record folly in the Old or the New
World anyhow, like my closet with its incredible
debris of cluttered old letters by the thousands,
books, dust, magazines, childhood boxscores, the
likes of which when I woke up the other night
from a pure sleep, made me groan to think this
is what I was doing with my waking hours: bur-
dening myself with junk neither I nor anybody
else should really want or will ever remember in
Heaven.

Anyway, an example of my troubles at the library. They didnt bring me those books. On open-
ing them I think they would have cracked apart.
What I really shoulda done is say to that head
librarian:– "I'm gonna put you in a horseshoe and
give you to a horse to wear in the Battle of
Chickamauga."

12.

MEANWHILE I KEPT ASKING EVERYBODY IN PARIS "Where's Pascal buried? Where's Balzac's cemetery?" Somebody finally told me Pascal must certainly be buried out of town at Port Royal near his pious sister, Jansenists, and as for Balzac's cemetery I didnt wanta go to no cemetery at midnight (Pere Lachaise) and anyway as we were blasting along in a wild taxi ride at 3 A.M. near Montparnasse they yelled "There's your Balzac! His statue on the square!"

"Stop the cab!" and I got out, swept off me hat in sweeping bow, saw the statue vaguely gray in the drunken misting streets, and that was that. And how could I find my way to Port Royal if I could hardly find my way back to my hotel?

And besides they're not there at all, only their bodies.

13.

PARIS IS A PLACE WHERE YOU CAN REALLY WALK around at night and find what you dont want, O Pascal.

Trying to make my way to the Opera a hundred cars came charging around a blind curve-corner and like all the other pedestrians I waited to let them pass and then they all started across but I waited a few seconds looking the other charging cars over, all coming from six directions—Then I stepped off the curb and a car came around that curve all alone like the chaser running last in a Monaco race and right at me—I stepped back just in time—At the wheel a Frenchman completely convinced that no one else has a right to live or get to his mistress as fast as he does—As a New Yorker I run to dodge the free zipping roaring traffic of Paris but Parisians just stand and then stroll and leave it to the driver—And by God it works, I saw dozens of cars screech to a stop from 70 M.P.H. to let some stroller have his way!

I was going to the Opera also to eat in any restaurant that looked nice, it was one of my sober evenings dedicated to solitary studious walks, but O what grim rainy Gothic buildings and me walking well in the middle of those wide sidewalks so's to avoid dark doorways—What vistas of Nowhere City Night and hats and umbrellas—I couldn't even buy a newspaper—Thousands of people were coming out of some performance somewhere—I went to a crowded restaurant on Boulevard des Italiens and sat way at the end of the bar by myself on a high stool and watched, wet and helpless, as waiters mashed up raw hamburg with Worcestershire sauce and other things and other waiters rushed by holding up steaming trays of good food—The one sympathetic counterman brought menu and Alsatian beer I ordered and I told him to wait awhile—He didnt understand that, drinking without eating at once, because he is partner to the secret of charming French eaters:— they rush at the very beginning with *hors d'oeuvres* and bread, and then plunge into their entrees (this is practically always before even a slug of wine) and then they slow down and start lingering, now the wine to wash the mouth, now comes the *talk,* and now the second half of the meal, wine, dessert and coffee, something I cannae do.

In any case I'm drinking my second beer and reading the menu and notice an American guy is sitting five stools away but he is so mean looking in his absolute disgust with Paris I'm afraid

to say "Hey, you American?"—He's come to
Paris expecting he woulda wound up under a
cherry tree in blossom in the sun with pretty girls
on his lap and people dancing around him, instead
he's been wandering the rainy streets alone in all
that jargon, doesnt even know where the whore
district is, or Notre Dame, or some small cafe
they told him about back in Glennon's bar on
Third Avenue, *nothing*—When he pays for his
sandwich he literally throws the money on the
counter "You wouldnt help me figure what the
real price is anyway, and besides shove it up your
you-know-what I'm going back to my old mine
nets in Norfolk and get drunk with Bill Eversole
in the bookie joint and all the other things you
dumb frogs dont know about," and stalks out in
poor misunderstood raincoat and disillusioned
rubbers—

Then in come two American schoolteachers of
Iowa, sisters on a big trip to Paris, they've apparently got a hotel room round the corner and
aint left it except to ride the sightseeing buses
which pick em up at the door, but they know this
nearest restaurant and have just come down to
buy a couple of oranges for tomorrow morning
because the only oranges in France are apparently
Valencias imported from Spain and too expensive
for anything so avid as quick simple *break* of
fast. So to my amazement I hear the first clear
bell tones of American speech in a week:– "You
got some oranges here?"

"*Pardon?*"—the counterman.

"There they are in that glass case," says the
other gal.

"Okay—see?" pointing, "two oranges," and showing two fingers, and the counterman takes out the two oranges and puts em in a bag and says crisply thru his throat with those Arabic Parisian "r's" :–

"*Trois francs cinquante.*" In other words, 35¢ an orange but the old gals dont care what it costs and besides they dont understand what he's said.

"What's *that* mean?"

"*Pardon?*"

"Alright, I'll hold out my palm and take your kwok-kowk-kwark out of it, all we want's the oranges" and the two ladies burst into peals of screaming laughter like on the porch and the cat politely removes three francs fifty centimes from her hand, leaving the change, and they walk out lucky they're not alone like that American guy—

I ask my counterman what's real good and he says Alsatian Choucroute which he brings—It's just hotdogs, potatos and sauerkraut, but such hotdogs as chew like butter and have a flavor delicate as the scent of wine, butter and garlic all cooking together and floating out a cafe kitchen door—The sauerkraut no better'n Pennsylvania, potatos we got from Maine to San Jose, but O yes I forgot:– with it all, on top, is a weird soft strip of bacon which is really like ham and is the best bite of all.

I had come to France to do nothing but walk and eat and this was my first meal and my last, ten days.

But in referring back to what I said to Pascal, as I was leaving this restaurant (paid 24 francs, or almost $5 for this simple platter) I heard a howling in the rainy boulevard—A maniacal Algerian had gone mad and was shouting at everyone and everything and was holding something I couldnt see, very small knife or object or pointed ring or something—I had to stop in the door—People hurried by scared—I didn't want to be *seen* by him hurrying away—The waiters came out and watched with me—He approached us stabbing outdoor wicker chairs as he came—The headwaiter and I looked calmly into each other's eyes as tho to say "Are we together?"—But my counterman began talking to the mad Arab, who was actually light haired and probably half French half Algerian, and it became some sort of conversation and I walked around and went home in a now-driving rain, had to hail a cab.

Romantic raincoats.

14.

IN MY ROOM I LOOKED AT MY SUITCASE SO CLEVERLY
packed for this big trip the idea of which began
all the previous winter in Florida reading Voltaire, Chateaubriand, de Montherlant (whose
latest book was even now displayed in the shop-
windows of Paris, "The Man Who Travels Alone
is a Devil")—Studying maps, planning to walk
all over, eat, find my ancestors' home town in the
Library and then go to Brittany where it was
and where the sea undoubtedly washed the rocks
—My plan being, after five days in Paris, go to
that inn on the sea in Finistère and go out at
midnight in raincoat, rain hat, with notebook and
pencil and with large plastic bag to write inside
of, i.e., stick hand, pencil and notebook into bag,
and write dry, while rain falls on rest of me, write
the sounds of the sea, part two of poem "Sea" to
be entitled: "SEA, Part Two, the Sounds of the

Atlantic at X, Brittany," either at outside of
Carnac, or Concarneau, or Pointe de Penmarch,
or Douardenez, or Plouzaimedeau, or Brest, or
St. Malo—There in my suitcase, the plastic bag,
the two pencils, the extra leads, the notebook, the
scarf, the sweater, the raincoat in the closet, and
the warm shoes—

The warm shoes indeed, I'd also brought Florida
air-conditioned shoes anticipating long hotsun
walks in Paris and hadnt worn them once, the
"warm shoes" were all I wore the whole blessed
time—In the Paris papers people were complain-
ing about the solid month of rain and cold
throughout late-May and early-June France as
being caused by scientists tampering with the
weather.

And my first aid kit, and my mittens for the
cold midnight musings on the Breton shore when
the writing's done, and all fancy sports shirts
and extra socks I never even got to wear in Paris
let alone London where I'd also planned to go,
not to mention Amsterdam and Cologne after-
wards.

I was already homesick.

Yet this book is to prove that no matter how
you travel, how "successful" your tour, or fore-
shortened, you always learn something and learn
to change your thoughts.

As usual I was simply concentrating everything in one intense but thousandéd "Ah-*ha*!"

15.

FOR INSTANCE THE NEXT AFTERNOON AFTER A GOOD sleep, and me spruced up clean again, I met a Jewish composer or something from New York, with his bride, and somehow they liked me and anyway they were lonely and we had dinner, the which I didnt touch much as I hit up on cognac neat again—"Let's go around the corner and see a movie," he says, which we do after I've talked a half dozen eager French conversations around the restaurant with Parisians, and the movie turns out to be the last few scenes of O'Toole and Burton in "Becket," very good, especially their meeting on the beach on horseback, and we say goodbye—

Again, I go into a restaurant right across from La Gentilhommière recommended to me highly by Jean Tassart, swearing this time I'll have a full course Paris dinner—I see a quiet man spoon-

ing a sumptuous soup in a huge bowl across the
way and order it by saying "The same soup as
Monsieur." It turns out to be a fish and cheese
and red pepper soup as hot as Mexican peppers,
terrific and *pink*—With this I have the fresh
French bread and gobs of creamery butter but
by the time they're ready to bring me the entree
chicken roasted and basted with champagne and
then sautéed in champagne, and the mashed sal-
mon on the side, the anchovie, the Gruyère, and
the little sliced cucumbers and the little tomatos
red as cherries and then by God actual fresh
cherries for dessert, all *mit* wine of vine, I have
to apologize I cant even think of eating anything
after all that (my stomach's shrunk by now, lost
15 pounds)—But the quiet soup gentleman moves
on to a broiled fish and we actually start chatting
across the restaurant and turns out he's the art
dealer who sells Arps and Ernsts around the
corner, knows André Breton, and wants me to
visit his shop tomorrow. A marvelous man, and
Jewish, and we have our conversation in French,
and I even tell him that I roll my "r's" on my
tongue and not in my throat because I come from
Medieval French Quebec-via-Brittany stock, and
he agrees, admitting that modern Parisian French,
tho dandy, *has* really been changed by the influx
of Germans, Jews and Arabs for all these two
centuries and not to mention the influence of the
fops in the court of Louis Fourteenth which really
started it all, and I also remind him that François
Villon's real name was pronounced "Ville On"
and not "Viyon" (which is a corruption) and that
in those days you said not "toi" or "moi" but like

"twé" or "mwé" (as we still do in Quebec and in
two days I heard it in Brittany) but I finally
warned him, concluding my charming lecture
across the restaurant as people listened half
amused and half attentive, François' name *was*
pronounced François and not Françwé for the
simple reason that he spelled it Françoy, like the
King is spelled Roy, and this has nothing to do
with "oi" and if the King had ever heard it pronounced rouwé (rwé) he would not have invited
you to the Versailles dance but given you a *roué*
with a hood over his head to deal with your im-
pertinent *cou*, or coup, and couped it right off and
recouped you nothing but loss.

Things like that—

Maybe that's when my Satori took place. Or
how. The amazing long sincere conversations in
French with hundreds of people everywhere, was
what I really liked, and did, and it was an ac-
complishment because they couldnt have replied
in detail to my detailed points if they hadnt understood every word I said. Finally I began being
so cocky I didn't even bother with Parisian French
and let loose blasts and *pataraffes* of *chalivarie*
French that had them in stitches because they
still understood, so there, Professor Sheffer and
Professor Cannon (my old French "teachers" in
college and prep school who used to laugh at my
"accent" but gave me A's.)

But enough of that.

Suffice it to say, when I got back to New York
I had more fun talking in Brooklyn accents'n I
ever had in me life and especially when I got
back down South, whoosh, what a miracle are

different languages and what an amazing Tower
of Babel this world is. Like, imagine going to
Moscow or Tokyo or Prague and listening to all
that.

That people actually understand what their
tongues are babbling. And that eyes do shine to
understand, and that responses are made which
indicate a soul in all this matter and mess of
tongues and teeth, mouths, cities of stone, rain,
heat, cold, the whole wooden mess all the way
from Neanderthaler grunts to Martian-probe
moans of intelligent scientists, nay, all the way
from the Johnny Hart ZANG of anteater tongues
to the dolorous *"la notte, ch'i' passai con tanta
pieta"* of Signore Dante in his understood shroud
of robe ascending finally to Heaven in the arms of
Beatrice.

Speaking of which I went back to see the
gorgeous young blonde in La Gentilhommière and
she piteously calls me "Jacques" and I have to
explain to her my name is "Jean" and so she sobs
her "Jean," grins, and leaves with a handsome
young boy and I'm left there hanging on the bar
stool pestering everybody with my poor loneliness
which goes unnoticed in the crashing busy night,
in the smash of the cash register, the racket of
washing glasses. I want to tell them that we dont
all want to become ants contributing to the social
body, but individualists each one counting one
by one, but no, try to tell that to the in-and-outers
rushing in and out the humming world night as
the world turns on one axis. The secret storm has
become a public tempest.

But Jean-Pierre Lemaire the Young Breton poet

is tending the bar, sad and handsome as none but
French youths can be, and very sympathetic with
my silly position as a visiting drunkard alone in
Paris, shows me a good poem about a hotel room
in Brittany by the sea but after that shows me a
meaningless surrealist-type poem about chicken
bones on some girl's tongue ("Take it back to
Cocteau!" I feel like yelling in English) but I
don't want to hurt him, and he's been nice but's
afraid to talk to me because he's on duty and
crowds of people are at the outdoor tables waiting
for their drinks, young lovers head to head, I'd-
a done better staying home and painting the
"Mystical Marriage of St. Catherine" after Gi-
rolamo Romanino but I'm so enslaved to yak and
tongue, paint bores me, and it takes a lifetime to
learn how to paint.

16.

I MEET MONSIEUR CASTLEJALOUX IN A BAR ACROSS
the street from church of St. Louis de France
and tell him about the library—He invites me to
the National Archives the next day and will see
what he can do—Guys are playing billiards in the
back room and I'm watching real close because
lately down South I've begun to shoot some real
good pool especially when I'm drunk, which is
another good reason to give up drinking, but they
pay absolutely no attention to me as I keep saying
"Bon!" (like an Englishman with handlebar
mustache and no front teeth yelling "Good Shot!"
in a clubroom)—Billiards with no pockets however not my meat—I like pockets, holes, I like
straightahead bank shots that are utterly impossible except with high inside-or-outside English,
just a slice, hard, the ball clocks in and the cue-
ball leaps up, one time it leaped up, rolled around

49

the edges of the table and bounced back on the
green and the game was over, as it was the eight-
ball slotted in— (A shot referred to by my Southern pool partner Cliff Anderson as a "Jesus Christ
shot")—Naturally, being in Paris I wanta play
some pool with the local talent and test Wits
Transatlantique but they're not interested—As
I say, I go to the National Archives on a curious
street called Rue de les Francs Bourgeois (you
might say, "street of the outspoken middleclass,")
surely a street you once saw old Balzac's floppy
coat go flapping down on an urgent afternoon to
his printer's galleys, or like the cobblestoned
streets of Vienna when once Mozart did walk
with floppy pants one afternoon on the way to his
librettist, coughing)—

I'm directed into the main office of the Archives
where Mr. Casteljaloux wears today a melancho-
lier look than the one he wore yesterday on his
clean handsome ruddy blue eyed middleaged face
—It tugs at my heart to hear him say that since
he saw me yesterday, his mother's fallen seriously
ill and he has to go to her now, his secretary will
take care of everything.

She is, as I say, that ravishingly beautiful, un-
forgettably raunchily edible Breton girl with seagreen eyes, blueblack hair, little teeth with the
slight front separation that, had she met a dentist
who proposed to straighten them out, every man
in the world shoulda strapped him to the neck
of the wooden horse of Troy to let him have one
look at captive Helen 'ere Paris beleaguered his
treacherous and lecherous Gaulois Gullet.

Wearing a white knit sweater, golden bracelets

and things, and perceiving me with her sea eyes,
I ayed and almost saluted but only admitted to
myself that such a woman were wronks and wars
and not for me the peaceful shepherd mit de
cognac—I'd a Eunuch been, to play with such
proclivities and declivities two weeks—

I suddenly longed to go to England as she began
to rattle off that there were only *manuscripts* in
the National Archives and a lot of them had been
burned in the Nazi bombing and besides they had
no records there of *"les affaires Colonielles"* (Colo-
nial matters).

"Colon*ielles!*" I yelled in a real rage glaring at
her.

"Dont you have a list of the officers in Montcalm's Army in 1756?" I went on, getting to the
point at least, but so mad at her for her Irish
haughtiness (yes *Irish*, because all Bretons came
from Ireland one way or the other before Gaul
was called Gaul and Caesar saw a Druid tree
stump and before Saxons showed up and before
and after Pictish Scotland and so on), but no,
she gives me that seagreen look and Ah, now I
see her—

"My ancestor was an officer of the Crown, his
name I just told you, and the year, he came from
Brittany, he was a Baron they tell me, I'm the
first of the family to return to France to look
for the records." But then I realized I was being
haughtier, nay, not haughtier than she was but
simpler than a street beggar to even talk like that
or even try to find any records, making true or
false, since as a Breton she probably knew it could
only be found in Brittany as there had been a

little war called *La Vendée* between Catholic Brittany and Republican Atheist Paris too horrible to
mention a stone's throw from Napoleon's tomb—

The main fact was, she'd heard M. Casteljaloux
tell her all about me, my name, my quest, and it
struck her as a silly thing to do, tho noble, noble
in the sense of hopeless noble *try*, because Johnny
Magee around the corner as anybody knows can,
with any luck, find in Ireland that he's the descendant of the Morholt's King and so what?
Johnny Anderson, Johnny Goldstein, Johnny Anybody, Lin Chin, Ti Pak, Ron Poodlewhorferer,
Anybody.

And for me, an American, to handle manuscripts there, if any relating to my problem, what
difference did it make?

I dont remember how I got out of there but the
lady was not pleased and neither was I—But
what I didnt know about Brittany at the time
was that Quimper, in spite of its being the
ancient capital of Cornouialles and the residence
of its kings or hereditary counts and latterly the
capital of the department of Finistère and all
that, was nevertheless of all dumb bigcity things
considered a hickplace by the popular wits of
Paris, because of its distance from the capital, so
that as you might say to a New York Negro "If
you dont do right I'm gonna send you back to
Arkansas," Voltaire and Condorcet would laugh
and say "If you dont understand aright we'll send
you out to Quimper ha ha ha."—Connecting that
with Quebec and the famous dumb Canucks she
musta laughed in her teeth.

I went, on somebody's tip, to the Bibliothèque

Mazarine near Quai St. Michel and nothing happened there either except the old lady librarian
winked at me, gave me her name (Madame Oury),
and told me to write to her anytime.

All there was to do in Paris was done.

I bought an air ticket to Brest, Brittany.

Went down to the bar to say goodbye to everybody and one of them, Goulet the Breton said,
"Be careful, they'll *keep* you there!"

p.s.   As one last straw, before buying the ticket,
I went over to my French publishers and announced my name and asked for the boss—The
girl either believed that I was one of the authors
of the house, which I am to the tune of six novels
now, or not, but she coldly said that he was out
to lunch—

"Alright then, where's Michel Mohrt?" (in
French) (my editor of sorts there, a Breton from
Lannion Bay at Louquarec.)

"He's out to lunch too."

But the fact of the matter was, he was in New
York that day but she couldnt care less to tell
me and with me sitting in front of this imperious
secretary who must've thought she was very
Madame Defarge herself in Dickens' "Tale of Two
Cities" sewing the names of potential guillotine
victims into the printer's cloth, were a half dozen
eager or worried future writers with their manuscripts all of whom gave me a positively dirty
look when they heard my name as tho they were
muttering to themselves "*Kerouac?* I can write
ten times better than that beatnik maniac and
I'll prove it with this here manuscript called
'Silence au Lips' all about how Renard walks into

the foyer lighting a cigarette and refuses to ac-
knowledge the sad formless smile of the plotless
Lesbian heroine whose father just died trying to
rape an elk in the Battle of Cuckamonga, and
Phillipe the intellectual enters in the next chapter
lighting a cigarette with an existential leap across
the blank page I leave next, all ending in a
monologue encompassing etc., all this Kerouac
can do is write stories, ugh"—"And in such bad
taste, not even one well-defined heroine in domino
slacks crucifying chickens for her mother with
hammer and nails in a 'Happening' in the kitchen"
—agh, all I feel like singing is Jimmy Lunceford's
old tune:

> "It aint watcha do
> It's the way atcha do it!"

But seeing the sinister atmosphere of "literature" all around me and the broad aint gonna get
my publisher to buzz me into his office for an
actual business chat, I get up and snarl:

"Aw shit, *j'm'en va à l'Angleterre*" (Aw shit,
I'm goin to England") but I should really have
said:

"*Le Petit Prince s'en va à la Petite Bretagne.*"

Means: "The Little Prince is going to Little
Britain" (or, Brittany.)

17.

OVER AT GARE ST.-LAZARE I BOUGHT AN AIR-INTER
ticket *one-way* to Brest (not heeding Goulet's advice) and cashed a travellers check of $50 (big
deal) and went to my hotel room and spent two
hours repacking so everything'd be alright and
checking the rug on the floor for any lints I
mighta left, and went down all dolled up (shaved
etc.) and said goodbye to the evil woman and
the nice man her husband who ran the hotel, with
my hat on now, the rain hat I intended to wear
on the midnight sea rocks, always wore it pulled
down over the left eye I guess because that's the
way I wore my pea cap in the Navy—There were
no great outcries of please come back but the
desk clerk observed me as tho he was like to try
me sometime.

Off we go in the cab to Orly airfield, in the
rain again, 10 A.M. now, the cab zipping with

beautiful speed out past all those signs advertising cognac and the surprising little stone country houses in between with French gardens of flowers and vegetables exquisitely kept, everything green as I imagine it must be in Auld England now.

(Like a nut I figured I could fly from Brest to London, only 150 miles as the crow flies.)

At Orly I check in my small but heavy suitcase at Air-Inter and then wander around till 12 noon boarding call. I drink cognac and beer in the really marvelous cafes they have in that air terminal, nothing so dismal as Idlewild Kennedy with its plush-carpet and cocktail-lounge Everybody-Quiet shot. For the second time I give a franc to the lady who sits in front of the toilets at a table, asking her: "Why do you sit there and why do people give you tips?"

"Because I *clean* the joint" which I understand right away and appreciate, thinking of my mother back home who has to *clean* the house while I yell insults at the T.V. from my rockingchair. So I say:

"Un franc pour la Française."

I coulda said "The Inferno White Owl Sainte Theresia!" and she still wouldna cared. (Wouldn't *have* cared, but I shorten things, after that great poet Robert Burns.)

So now it's "Mathilda" I'm singing because the bell-tone announcing flights sings just like that song, in Orly, "Ma – Thil – Daa" and the quiet girlvoice: "Pan American Airlines Flight 603 to Karachi now loading at gate 32" or "K.L.M. Royal Dutch Airlines Flight 709 to Johannesburg now loading at gate 49" and so on, what an airport, people hear me singing "Mathilda" all over the

place and I've already had a long talk about dogs
with two Frenchmen and a dachsund in the cafe,
and now I hear: "Air-Inter Flight 3 to Brest now
loading at gate 96" and I start walking—down a
long smooth corridor—

I walk about I swear a quartermile and come
practically to the end of the terminal building and
there's Air-Inter, a two-engined old B-26 I guess
with worried mechanics all fiddling around the
propeller on the port side—

It's flight time, noon, but I ask the people there
"What's wrong?"

"One hour delay."

There's no toilet here, no cafe, so I go back all
the way to while away the hour in a cafe, and
wait—

I go back at one.

"Half hour delay."

I decide to sit it out, but suddenly I have to go
to the toilet at 1:20—I ask a Spanish-looking
Brest-bound passenger: "Think I got time to go
to the toilet back at the terminal?"

"O sure, plenty time."

I look, the mechanics out there are still wor-
riedly fiddling, so I hurry that quartermile back,
to the toilet, lay another franc for fun on La
Française, and suddenly I hear "Ma – Thil – Daa"
singsong with the word "Brest" so I like Clark
Gable's best fast walk hike on back almost as fast
as a jogging trackman, if you know what I mean,
but by the time I get there the plane is out taxi-
ing to the runway, the ramp's been rolled back
which all those traitors just crept up, and off they
go to Brittany with my suitcase.

18.

NOW I'M SUPPOSED TO GO DABBLING ALL OVER France with clean fingernails and a joyous tourist expression.

"*Calvert!*" I blaspheme at the desk (for which I'm sorry, Oh Lord). "I'm going to follow them in a train! Can you sell me a train ticket? They took off with my valise!"

"You'll have to go to Gare Montparnasse for that but I'm really sorry, Monsieur, but that is the most ridiculous way to miss a plane."

I say to myself "Yeah, you cheapskates, why dont you build a toilet."

But I go in a taxi 15 miles back to Gare Montparnasse and I buy a one-way ticket to Brest, first class, and as I think about my suitcase, and what Goulet said, I also remember now the pirates of St. Malo not to mention the pirates of Penzance.

Who cares? I'll catch up with the rats.

I get on the train among thousands of people, turns out there's a holiday in Brittany and everybody's going home.

There are those compartments where firstclass ticketed people can sit, and those narrow window alleys where secondclass ticketed people stand leaning at the windows and watch the land roll by—I pass the first compartment of the coach I picked and see nothing but women and babies—I know instinctively I'll choose the second compartment—And I do! Because what do I see in there but *"Le Rouge et le Noire"* (The Red and the Black), that is to say, the Military and the Church, a French soldier and a Catholic priest, and not only that but two pleasant looking old ladies and a weird looking drunklooking guy in the corner, that makes five, leaving the sixth and last place for me, "Jean-Louis Lebris de Kerouac" as I presently announce, knowing I'm home and they'll understand my family picked up some weird manners in Canada and the U.S.A.—(which I announce of course only after I've asked *"Je peu m'assoir?"* (I can sit?), "Yes," and I excuse myself across the ladies' legs and plump right down next to the priest, removed my hat already, and address him: *"Bonjour, mon Père."*

Now this is the real way to go to Brittany, gents.

19.

BUT THE POOR LITTLE PRIEST, DARK, SHALL WE SAY swart, or *swartz,* and very small and thin, his hands are trembling as if from ague and for all I know from Pascalian ache for the equation of the Absolute or maybe Pascal scared him and the other Jesuits with his bloody "Provincial Letters," but in any case I look into his dark brown eyes, I see his weird little parroty understanding of everything and of me too, and I pound my collarbone with my finger and say:

"I'm Catholic too."

He nods.

"I wear the Sacred Queen and also St. Benedict."

He nods.

He is such a little guy you could blow him away with one religious yell like *"O Seigneur!"* (Oh Lord!)

But now I turn my attention to the civilian in the corner, who's eyeing me with the exact eyes of an Irishman I know called Jack Fitzgerald and the same mad thirsty leer as tho he's about to say "Alright, where's the booze hidden in that raincoat of yours" but all he does say is, in French:

"Take off your raincoat, put it up on the rack."

Excusing myself as I have to bump knees with the blond soldier, and the soldier grins sadly ('cause I rode in trains with Aussies across wartime England 1943) I shove the lump of coat up, smile at the ladies, who just wanta get home the hell with all the characters, and I say my name to the guy in the corner (like I said I would).

"Ah, that's Breton. You live in Rennes?"

"No I live in Florida in America but I was born etc. etc." the whole long story, which interests them, and then I ask the guy's name.

It's the beautiful name of Jean-Marie Noblet.

"Is that Breton?"

"*Mais oui.*" (But yes.)

I think: "Noblet, Goulet, Havet, Champsecret, sure a lot of funny spellings in this country" as the train starts up and the priest settles down in a sigh and the ladies nod and Noblet eyes me like he would like to wink me a proposal that we get on with the drinking, a long trip ahead.

So I say "Let's you and I go buy some in the *commissaire.*"

"If you wanta try, okay."

"What's wrong?"

"Come on, you'll see."

And sure enough we have to rush weaving without bumping anybody through seven coaches of

packed windowstanders and on through the roaring swaying vestibules and jump over pretty girls
sitting on books on the floor and avoid collisions
with mobs of sailors and old country gentlemen
and all the lot, a homecoming holiday train like
the Atlantic Coast Line going from New York to
Richmond, Rocky Mount, Florence, Charleston,
Savannah and Florida on the Fourth of July or
Christmas and everybody bringing gifts like
Greeks beware we not of—

But me and old Jean-Marie find the liquor man
and buy two bottles of rosé wine, sit on the floor
awhile and chat with some guy, then catch the
liquor man as he's coming back the other way and
almost empty, buy two more, become great friends,
and rush back to our compartment feeling great,
high, drunk, wild—And don't you think we didnt
swing infos back and forth in French, and not
Parisian either, and him not speaking a word of
English.

I didnt even have a chance to look out the
window as we passed the Chartres Cathedral with
the dissimilar towers one five hundred years
older'n the other.

20.

WHAT GETS ME IS THAT, AFTER AN HOUR NOBLET
and I were waving our wine bottles across the poor
priest's face as we argued religion, history, politics, so suddenly I turned to him trembling there
and asked: "Do you mind our wine bottles?"

He gave me a look as if to say: "You mean that
lil ole winemaker me? No, no, I have a cold, you
see, I feel awful sick."

"*Il est malade, il à un rheum,*" (He's sick, he's
got a cold) I told Noblet grandly. The Soldier was
laughing all the while.

I said grandly to them all (and the English
translation is beneath this) :– "*Jésu à été cru-
cifié parce que, a place d'amenez l'argent et le
pouvoir, il à amenez seulement l'assurance que
l'existence à été formez par le Bon Dieu et elle
appartiens au Bon Dieu le Pêre, et Lui, le Pêre,
va nous élever au Ciel après la mort, ou parsonne*

63

n'aura besoin d'argent ou de pouvoir parce que
ça c'est seulement après tout d'la poussière et de
la rouille—Nous autres qu'ils n'ont pas vue les
miracles de Jésu, comme les Juifs et les Romans
et la 'tites poignée d'Grecs et d'autres de la riviêre
Nile et Euphrates, on à seulement de continuer
d'accepter l'assurance qu'il nous à été descendu
dans la parole sainte du nouveau testament—C'est
pareille comme ci, en voyant quelqu'un, on dira
'c'est pas lui, c'est pas lui!' sans savoir QUI est
lui, et c'est seulement le Fils qui connaient le Père
—Alors, la Foi, et l'Église qui à défendu la Foi
comme qu'a pouva." (Partly French Canuck.)
IN ENGLISH:– "Jesus was crucified because, instead of bringing money and power, He only
brought the assurance that existence was created
by God and it belongs to God the Father, and He,
the Father, is going to elevate us to Heaven after
death, where no one will need money or power
because that's only after all dust and rust—We
who have not seen the Miracles of Jesus, like the
Jews and the Romans and the little handful of
Greeks and others from the Nile River and the
Euphrates, only have to continue accepting the
assurance which has been handed down to us
in the Holy Writ of the New Testament—It's just
as though, on seeing someone, we'd say 'It's not
him, it's not him!' without knowing WHO he is,
and it's only the Son who knows the Father—
Therefore, Faith, and the Church which defended
the Faith as well as it could."

No applause from the priest, but a side underlook, brief, like the look of an applauder, thank
God.

21.

WAS THAT MY SATORI, THAT LOOK, OR NOBLET?
In any case it grew dark and when we got to
Rennes, in Brittany now, and I saw soft cows out
in the meadows blue dark near the rail, Noblet,
against the advice of the *farceurs* (jokesters) of
Paris advised me not to stay in the same coach,
but change to three coaches ahead, because the
trainmen were gonna make a cut and leave me
right there (headed, really, however, for my real
ancestral country, Cornouialles and environs) but
the trick was to get to Brest.

He led me off the train, after the others, and
walked me down the steaming station platform,
stopped me at a liquor man so I could buy me a
flask of cognac for the rest of the ride, and said
goodbye: he was home, in Rennes, and so was
the priest and the soldier, Rennes the former
capital of all Brittany, seat of an Archbishop,

headquarters of the 10th Army Corps, with the university and many schools, but not the real deep Brittany because in 1793 it was the headquarters of the Republican Army of the French Revolution against the Vendéans further in. And has ever since then been made the tribunal watchdog over those wild dog places. La Vendée, the name of the war between those two forces in history, was this:– the Bretons were against the Revolutionaries who were atheists and headcutters for fraternal reasons, while the Bretons had paternal reasons to keep to their old way of life.

Nothing to do with Noblet in 1965 A.D.

He disappeared into the night like a Céline character but what's the use of similes when discussing a gentleman's departure, and high as a noble at that, but not as drunk as me.

We'd come 232 miles from Paris, had 155 to go to Brest (end, *finis*, land, *terre*, Finistère), all the sailors still on board the train as naturally, as I didnt know, Brest is a Naval Base where Chateaubriand heard the booming cannons and saw the fleet come in triumphant from some fight in 1770's sometime.

My new compartment is just a young mother with a cantankerous baby daughter, and some guy I guess her husband, and I just occasionally sip my cognac then go out in the alleyway to look out the window at passing darkness with lights, a lone granite farmhouse with lights on just downstairs in the kitchen, and vague hints of hills and moors.

Clickety clack.

22.

I GET PRETTY FRIENDLY WITH THE YOUNG COUPLE
and at St. Brieuc the trainman yells out " S a i n t
B r r i e u !"—I yell out "Saint Brieuck!"

Trainman, seeing nobody's getting much off or
on, the lonely platform, repeats, advising me how
to pronounce these Breton names: "Saint Brrieu!"

"Saint Brieuck!" I yell, emphasizing as you see
the "c" noise of the thing there.

"Saint Brrieu!"

"Saint Brieuck!"

"Saint Brrieu!"

"Saint Brrieuck!"

"Saint Brrrieu!"

"Saint Brrrieuck!"

Here he realizes he's dealing with a maniack
and quits the game with me and it's a wonder I
didn't get thrown off the train right there on the
wild shore here called Coasts of the North (Côtes

du Nord) but he didnt even bother, after all the
Little Prince had his firstclass ticket and Little
Prick more likely.

But that was funny and I still insist, when
you're in Brittany (Armorica the ancient name),
land of Kelts, pronounce your "K's" with a *kuck*
—And as I've said elsewhere, if "Celts" were
pronounced with a soft "s" sound, as the Anglo-
Saxons deem to do, my name would sound like
this: (and other names) :–

    Jack Serouac
    Johnny Sarson
    Senator Bob Sennedy
    Hopalong Sassidy
    Deborah Serr (or Sarr)
    Dorothy Silgallen
    Mary Sarney
    Sid Simpleton
        and the
            Stone Monuments of Sarnac via Sornwall.

And anyway there's a place in Cornwall called
St. Breock, and we all know how to pronounce
that.

We finally arrive in Brest, end of the line, no
more land, and I help the wife and husband out
holding their portable crib thing—And there she
is, grim misting fog, strange faces looking at the
few passengers getting off, a distant hoot of a
boat, and a grim cafe across the street where
Lord I'll get no sympathy, I've come to trapdoor
Brittany.

Cognacs, beers, and then I ask where's the
hotel, right across the construction field—To my

left, stone wall overlooking grass. and sudden
drops and dim houses—Foghorn out there—The
Atlantic's bay and harbor—

Where's my suitcase? asks the desk man in the
grim hotel, why it's in the air line office I guess—

No rooms.

Unshaven, in a black raincoat with rain hat,
dirty, I walk outa there and go sploopsing up dark
streets looking like any decent American Boy in
trouble, old or young, for the Main Drag—I in-
stantly recognize it for what it is, Rue de Siam,
named after the King of Siam when he visited
here on some dull visit certainly grim too and
probably ran back to his tropical canaries as quick
as he could since the new mason breastworks of
Colbert certainly dont inspire no hope in the heart
of a Buddhist.

But I'm not a Buddhist, I'm a Catholic revisit-
ing the ancestral land that fought for Catholicism
against impossible odds yet won in the end, as
certes, at dawn, I'll hear the tolling of the *tocsin*
churchbells for the dead.

I hit for the brightest looking bar on Rue de
Siam which is a main street like the ones you
used to see, say, in the 40's, in Springfield Mass.,
or Redding Calif., or that main street James Jones
wrote about in "Some Came Running" in Illinois—

The owner of the bar is behind his cash register
doping out the horses at Longchamps—I immediately talk, tell him my name, his name is Mr.
Quéré (which reminds me of the spelling of
Québec) and he lets me sit and goof and drink
there all I want—Meanwhile the young bartender
is also glad to talk to me, has apparently heard

of my books, but after awhile (and just like Pierre LeMaire in La Gentilhommière) he suddenly stiffens, I guess from a sign from the boss, too much work to do, wash your glasses in the sink, I've outworn me welcome in another bar—

I've seen that expression on my father's face, a kind of disgusted lip-on-lip WHAT'S-THE-USE phooey, or ploof, (dédain) or plah, as he either walked away a loser from a racetrack or out of a bar where he didn't like what happened, and elsetimes, especially when thinking of history and the world, but that's when I walked out of that bar when that expression came over my own face—And the owner, who'd been really warm for a half hour, returned his attention to his figures with the sly underlook of after all a busy patron anywhere—But something had swiftly changed. (Gave my name for the first time.)

Their directions given to me for to find a hotel room did not evolve or *de*-volve me an actual brick and concrete place with a bed inside for me to lay my head in.

Now I was wandering in the very dark, in the fog, everything was closing down. Hoodlums roared by in small cars and some on motorcycles. Some stood on corners. I asked everybody where there was a hotel. Now they didnt even know. Gettin on 3 A.M. Groups of hoodlums came and went across the street from me. I say "hoodlums" but with everything closed, the final music joint already discharging a few wrangling customers who bellowed confusedly around cars, what was left i' the streets?

Miraculously, yet, I suddenly passed a band of

twelve or so Naval inductees who were singing a
martial song in chorus on the foggy corner. I went
right up to em, looked at the head singer, and with
me alcoholic hoarse baritone went "A a a a a a h"
—They waited—

"V é é é é "

They wondered who this nut was.

"M a h – r e e e e e – ee — ee — aaaah !"

Ah, *Ave Maria,* on the next notes I knew not the
words but just sang the melody and they caught
on, caught up the tune, and there we were a
chorus with baritone and tenors singing like sad
angels suddenly slowly—And right through the
whole first chorus—In the foggy foggy dew—
Brest Brittany—Then I said "Adieu" and walked
away. They never said a word.

Some nut with a raincoat and a hat.

23.

WELL, WHY DO PEOPLE CHANGE THEIR NAMES?
Have they done anything bad, are they criminals,
are they ashamed of their real names? Are they
afraid of something? Is there any law in America
against using your own real name?

I had come to France and Brittany just to look
up this old name of mine which is just about three
thousand years old and was never changed in all
that time, as who would change a name that
simply means House (Ker), In the Field (Ouac)—

Just as you say Camp (Biv), In the Field
(Ouac) (unless "bivouac" is the incorrect spelling of an old Bismarck word, silly to say that
because "bivouac" was a word used long before
1870 Bismarck)—the name Kerr, or Carr, simply
means *House*, why bother with a field?

I knew that the name of Cornish Celtic Language is Kernuak. I knew that there are stone

monuments called dolmens (tables of stone) at
Kériaval in Carnac, some called alignments at
Kermario, Kérlescant and Kérdouadec, and a town
nearby called Kéroual, and I knew that the
original name for Bretons was "Breons" (i.e.,
the Breton is *Le Breon*) and that I had an addi-
tive name "Le Bris" and here I was in "Brest"
and did this make me a Cimbric spy from the stone
monuments of Riestedt in Germany? Rietstap also
the name of the German who painstakingly com-
piled names of families and their scocheons and
had my family included in "Rivista Araldica"?
—You say I'm a snob?—I only wanted to find out
why my family never changed their name and
perchance find a tale there, and trace it back to
Cornwall, Wales, and Ireland and maybe Scotland
afore that I'm sure, then down over to the St.
Lawrence River city in Canada where I'm told
there was a Seigneurie (a Lordship) and therefore I can go live there (along with my thousands
of bowlegged French Canadian cousins bearing
the same name) and *never pay taxes*!

Now what redblooded American with a Pontiac,
a big mortgage and ulcers at March-time is not
interested in this great adventure!

Hey! I should've also sang to the Navy boys:

> "I joined the Navy
> To see the world
> And whaddid I see?
> I saw the sea."

24.

NOW I'M GETTING SCARED, I SUSPECT SOME OF THOSE guys crisscrossing the streets in front of my wandering path are fixing to mug me for my two or three hundred bucks left—It's foggy and still except for sudden squeek wheels of cars loaded with guys, no girls now—I get mad and go up to an apparent elderly printer hurrying home from work or cardgame, maybe my father's ghost, as surely my father musta looked down on me that night in Brittany at last where he and all his brothers and uncles and their fathers had all longed to go, and only poor Ti Jean finally made it and poor Ti Jean with his Swiss Army knife in the suitcase locked in an airfield twenty miles away across the moors—He, Ti Jean, threatened now not by Bretons, as on those tourney mornings when flags and public women made fight an honorable thing I guess, but in Apache alleys the slur

of Wallace Beery and worse than that of course, a
thin mustache and a thin blade or a small nickel
plated gun—No garrottes please, I've got my
armor on, my Reichian character armor that is
—How easy to joke about it as I scribble this
4,500 miles away safe at home in old Florida with
the doors locked and the Sheriff doin his best in
a town at least as bad but not as foggy and so
dark—

I keep looking over my shoulder as I ask the
printer "Where are the gendarmes?"

He hurries past me thinking it's just a lead-in
question to mug him.

On Rue de Siam I ask a young guy *"Ou sont les
gendarmes, leurs offices?"* (Where are the gendarmes, their office?)

"Dont you want a cab?" (in French).

"To go where? There are no hotels?"

"The police station is down Siam here, then left
and you'll see it."

"Merci, Monsieur."

I go down believing he gave me another bum
steer as he's in cahoots with the hoodlums, I turn
left, look over my shoulder, things have gotten
suddenly mighty quiet, and I see a building blur-
ring lights in the fog, the back of it, that I figure
is the police station.

I listen. Not a sound anywhere. No screeching
tires, no mumble voices, no sudden laughs.

Am I crazy? Crazy as that raccoon in Big Sur
Woods, or the sandpiper thereof, or any Olsky-
Polsky Sky Bum, or Route Sixty Six Silly Ele-
phant Eggplant Sycophant and with more to come.

I walk right into the precinct, take my Ameri-

can green passport from out my breast pocket,
present it to the gendarme desk sergeant and tell
him I cannot wander these streets all night without a room, etc., have money for a room etc., suitcase locked up etc., missed my plane etc., am a
tourist etc. and I am afearéd.

He understood.

His boss came out, the lieutenant I guess, they
made a few calls, got a car out front, I stuck 50
francs at the desk sergeant saying "Merci beau-
coup."

He shook his head.

It was one of the only three bills I had left in
my pocket (50 francs is worth $10) and when I
reached into my pocket I thought maybe it was
one of the 5 franc notes, or a ten, in any case the
fifty came out like when you draw a card anyway,
and I felt ashamed to think I was trying to bribe
them, it was only a tip—But you dont "tip" the
police of France.

In fact this *was* the Republican Army defending
a descendant of the Vendéan Bretons caught without his trapdoor.

Like the 20 centimes in St. Louis de France that
I shoulda stuck in the poorbox, as gold of the real
Caritas, I really could have dropped it on the sta-
tionhouse floor as I went out but how can such a
thought spontaneously enter the head of a crafty
worthless Canuck like me?

Or if the thought had entered my mind, would
they cry bribe?

No—the Gendarmes of France have a school of
their own.

25.

THIS COWARDLY BRETON (ME) WATERED DOWN BY
two centuries in Canada and America, nobody's
fault but my own, this Kerouac who would be
laughed at in Prince of Wales Land because he
cant even hunt, or fish, or fight a beef for his
fathers, this boastful, this prune, this rage and
rake and rack of lacks, "this trunk of humours"
as Shakespeare said of Falstaff, this false staff not
even a prophet let alone a knight, this fear-of-
death tumor, with tumescences in the bathroom,
this runaway slave of football fields, this strikeout
artist and base thief, this yeller in Paris salons
and mum in Breton fogs, this farceur jokester at
art galleries of New York and whimperer at police stations and over longdistance telephones, this
prude, this yellowbellied aide-de-campe with port-
folio full of port and folios, this pinner of flowers

and mocker at thorns, this very *Hurracan* like the gasworks of Manchester and Birmingham both, this ham, this tester of men's patience and ladies' panties, this boneyard of decay eating at rusty horse shoes hoping to win a game from . . . This, in short, scared and humbled dumbhead loud-mouth with-the-shits descendant of man.

The gendarmes have a school of their own, meaning, they dont accept bribes or tips, they say with their eyes: "To each his own, you with your fifty francs, me with my honorable civic courage —and civil at that."

Boom, he drives me to a little Breton inn on Rue Victor Hugo.

26.

A HAGGARD GUY LIKE ANY IRISHMAN COMES OUT
and tightens his bathrobe at the door, listens to
the gendarmes, okay, leads me into the room next
to the desk which I guess is where guys bring
their girls for a quickie, unless I'm wrong and
taking off again on joking about life—The bed is
perfect with seventeen layers of blankets over
sheets and I sleep for three hours and suddenly
they're yelling and scrambling for breakfast again
with shouts across courtyards, bing, bang, clatter
of pots and shoes dropping on the second floor,
cocks crowing, it's France and morning—

I gotta see it and anyway I cant sleep and
where's my cognac!

I wash my teeth with my fingers at the little
sink and rub my hair with my fingertips wishing
I had my suitcase and step out in the inn like that
looking for the toilet naturally. There's old Inn-

keeper, actually a young guy 35 and a Breton, I forgot or omitted to ask his name, but he doesnt care how wildhaired I am and that the gendarmes had to find me a room, "There's the toilet, first right."

"La Poizette ah?" I yell.

He gives me the look that says "Get in the toilet and shut up."

When I come out I am trying to get to my sink in my room to comb my hair but he's already got breakfast coming for me in the diningroom where nobody is but us—

"Wait, comb my hair, get my cigarettes, and, ah, how about a beer first?"

"Wa? You crazy? Have your coffee first, your bread and butter."

"Just a little beer."

"AWright, awright, just one—Sit here when you get back, I've got work to do in the kitchen."

But this is all spoken that fast and even, but in Breton French which I dont have to make an effort like I do in Parisian French, to enunciate: just: *"Ey, weyondonc, pourquoi t'a peur que j'm'dégrise avec une 'tite bierre?"* (Hey, come on, how come you're scared of me sobering up with a little beer?)

"On s'dégrise pas avec la bierre, Monsieur, mais avec le bon petit déjeuner." (We dont sober up with beer, Monsieur, but with a nice breakfast.)

"Way, mais on est pas toutes des soulons." (Yah, but not everybody's a drunk.)

"Dont talk like that Monsieur. It's there, look, here, in the good Breton butter made with cream, and bread fresh from the baker, and strong hot coffee, that's how we sober up—Here's your beer, voila, I'll keep the coffee hot on the stove."

"Good! Now there's a real man."

"You speak the good French but you have an accent—?"

"*Oua, du Canada.*"

"Ah yes, because your passport is American."

"But I havent learned French in books but at home, I didnt know how to speak English in America before I was, oh, five six years old, my parents were born in Canada in Québec, the name of my mother is L'Évêsque."

"Ah, that's Breton also."

"But why, I thought it was Norman."

"Well Norman, Breton—"

"This and that—the French of the North in any case, ahn?"

"*Ah oui.*"

I pour myself a creamlike head over my beer out of the bottle of Alsatian beer, the best i' the west, as he watches disgusted, in his apron, he has rooms to clean upstairs, what's this dopey American Canuck hanging him up for and why does this always happen to him?

I say to him my full name and he yawns and says "*Way*, there are a lot of Lebris' here in Brest, coupla dozen. This morning before you got up a party of Germans had a great breakfast right where you're sittin there, they're gone now."

"They had fun in Brest?"

"*Cer*tainly! You've got to stay! You only got here yesterday—"

"I'm going to Air-Inter get my valise and I'm going to England, today."

"But"—he looks at me helplessly—"you havent seen Brest!"

I said "Well, if I can come back here tonight and sleep I can stay in Brest, after all I've gotta have *some* place" ("I may not be an experienced German tourist," I add to think to myself, "not having toured Brittany in 1940 but I certainly know some boys in Massachusetts who toured it for you outa the St. Lo breakthrough in 1944, I do") ("and French Canadian boys at that.")— And that's that, because he says:–

"Well I may not have a room for you tonight, and then again I may, all depends, Swiss parties are coming."

("And Art Buchwald," I thought.)

He said: "Now eat your good Breton butter." The butter was in a little clay butter bucket two inches high and so wide and so cute I said:–

"Let me have this butter bucket when I've finished the butter, my mother will love it and it will be a souvenir for her from Brittany."

"I'll get you a clean one from the kitchen. Meanwhile you eat your breakfast and I'll go upstairs and make a few beds" so I slup down the rest of the beer, he brings the coffee and rushes upstairs, and I smur (like Van Gogh's butterburls) fresh creamery butter outa that little bucket, almost all of it in one bite, right on the fresh bread, and crunch, munch, talk about your Fritos, the butter's gone even before Krupp and Remington got up to stick a teaspoon smallsize into a butler-cut-up grapefruit.

Satori there in Victor Hugo Inn?

When he comes down, nothing's left but me and

one of those wild powerful Gitane (means Gypsy) cigarettes and smoke all over.

"Feel better?"

"Now that's butter—the bread extraspecial, the coffee strong and exquisite—But now I desire my cognac."

"Well pay your room bill and go down rue Victor Hugo, on the corner is cognac, go get your valise and settle your affairs and come back here find out if there's a room tonight, beyond that old buddy old Neal Cassady cant go no further. To each his own and I got a wife and kids upstairs so busy playing with flowerpots, if, why if I had a thousand Syrians racking the place in Nominoé's own brown robes, they'd still let me do all the work, as it is, as you know, a hard-net Keltic sea." (I ingrained his thought there for your delectation, and if you didnt like it, call it beanafaction, in other words I beaned ya with my high hard one.)

I say "Where's Plouzaimedeau? I wanta write poems by the side of the sea at night."

"Ah you mean Plouzémédé—Ah, spoff, not my affair—I gotta work now."

"Okay I'll go."

But as an example of a regular Breton, aye?

27.

So I GO DOWN TO THE CORNER BAR AS DIRECTED AND walk in and there's old Papa Bourgeois or more likely Kervélégan or Ker-thisser and Ker-thatter behind the bar, gives me a cold gyrene look gyring me wide around and I say "Cognac, Monsieur." He takes his bloody time. A young mailman walks in with his leather shoulder-hanging pouch and starts in talking to him. I take my delicate cognac to a table and sit and on the first sip I shudder to miss what I missed all night. (They had some brands there besides Hennessey and Courvoisier and Monnet, that musta been why Winston Churchill that old Baron crying for his hounds in his weird wield weir, was always in France with cigar-a-mouth painting.) The owner eyes me narrowly. Clearly. I go up to the mailman and say: "Where's the office in town of the Air-Inter airplane company?"

"No savvy." (but in French).

"You a mailman in Brest and dont even know where an important office is?"

"What's so important about it?"

("Well for one thing," I say to myself to him extra-sensorily, "it's the only way you can get outa here—*fast*.") But all I say is: "My suitcase is there and I'm gonna get it back."

"Gee I dont know where it is. Do *you*, boss?"

No answer.

I said "Okay, I'll find it myself" and finished my cognac, and the mailman said:

"I am only a *facteur*" (mailman).

I said something to him in French which is published in heaven, which I insist to print here only in French: *"Tu travaille avec la maille pi tu sais seulement pas s'qu'est une office—d'importance?"*

"I'm new on the job" he said in French.

I'm not trying to belabor no point but listen to this:—

It's not my fault, or that of any American tourist or even patriot, that the French refuse the responsibility of their explanations—It's their right to demand privacy, but farcing is submittable to a court of Law, O Monsieur Bacon et Monsieur Coke—Farcing, or deceit, is submittable to a court of Law when it concerns your loss of civil welfare or safety.

It's as tho some Negro tourist like Papa Kane of Senegal came up to me on the sidewalk on Sixth Avenue and 34th street and asked me which way to the Dixie Hotel on Times Square, and instead I directed him to the Bowery, where he would (let's say) be killed by Basque and Indian

muggers, and a witness heard me give this innocent African tourist these wrong directions, and
then testified in court that he heard these *farcing*
instructions with intent to deprive of right-of-
way, or right-of-social-way or right-of-proper-
direction, then let's blast all the uncooperative and
unmannerly divisionist rats on both sides of
Spoofism and other Isms too anyway.

But the old owner of the bar quietly tells me
where it is and I thank him and go.

28.

NOW I SEE THE HARBOR, THE FLOWERPOTS IN BACK
of kitchens, old Brest, the boats, coupla tankers out
there, and the wild headlands in the gray scud-
ding sky, summat like Nova Scotia.

I find the office and go in. Here's two characters
in there involved with onionskinned duplicated
copies of everything and not even a mistress on
their knee, tho she's in back right now. I put
points, papers, down, they say wait an hour. I say
I wanta fly to London tonight. They say Air-Inter
doesnt fly direct to London but back to Paris and
you gets another company. ("Brest is only a you-
know-what-hair from Cornwall," I wish I could
tell them, "why fly back to Paris?") "Alright, so
I'll fly to Paris. What time today?"

"Not today. Monday is the next flight from
Brest."

I can just picture myself hanging around Brest

for one jolly whole weekend with no hotel room
and no one to talk to. Right then a gleam comes
in my eye as I think: "It's Saturday morning, I
can be in Florida in time for the funnies at dawn
when the guy placks em on my driveway!"—"Is
there a train back to Paris?"

"Yes, at three."

"Sell me a ticket?"

"You have to go there yourself."

"And my suitcase again?"

"Wont be here till noon."

"So I go buy ticket at railroad station, talk to
Stepin Fetchit awhile and call him Old Black Joe,
and even sing it, give him French kiss, peck on
each cheek, give him quarter, and come back
here."

I didnt actually say that but I shoulda but I
only said "Okay" and went down the station, got
the firstclass ticket, came back the same way, by
now already an expert on Brest streets, looked in,
no suitcase yet, went to Rue de Siam, cognac and
beer, dull, came back, no suitcase, so went into the
bar next door to this Air Office of the Breton Air
Force which I should write long letters to Mac-
Mullen of SAC about—

I know there are a lot of beautiful churches and
chapels out there that I should go look at, and then
England, but since England's in my heart why go
there? and 'sides, it doesnt matter how charming
cultures and art are, they're useless without sympathy—All the prettiness of tapestries, lands,
people:– *worthless* if there is no sympathy—Poets
of genius are just decorations on the wall if without the poetry of kindness and Caritas—This

means that Christ was right and everybody since then (who "thought" and wrote opposing views of their own) (like, say, Sigmund Freud and his cold depreciation of helpless personalities), was *wrong* —in that, the life of a person is, as W. C. Fields says, "Fraught with eminent peril" but when you know that when you die you will be elevated because you've done no harm, Ah take that back to Brittany and Elsewhere too—Do we need a Definition-of-Harm University to teach this? Let no man impel you to evil. The Guardian of Purgatory has the two Keys to St. Peter's Gate and himself's the third and deciding key.

And you impel no one to evil, or you shall have your balls of your eyes and the rest roasted like at an Iroquois stake and by the Devil himself, he who chose Judas for his chews. (Outa Dante.)

Whatever wrong you do shall be returned to you a hundredfold, jot and tittle, by the laws that operate in what science now calls "the deepening mystery of research."

Well re-search this, Creighton, by the time yore investigations are complete, the Hound Dog of Heaven'll take you straight to Massah.

29.

So I go into that bar so's not to miss my suitcase with its blessed belongings, as if like Joe
E. Lewis the comedian I could try to take my
things to Heaven with me, while you're alive on
earth the very hairs of your cats on your clothes
are blessed, and later on we can all gape and yaw
at Dinosaurs together, well, here's this bar and I
go in, sip awhile, go back two doors, the suitcase's
there at last and tied to a chain.

The clerks say nothing, I pick up the suitcase
and the chain falls off. Naval cadets in there buying tickets stare as I lift the suitcase. I show them
my name written in orange paint on a black tape
strip near the keyhole. My name. I walk out,
with it.

I lug the suitcase into Fournier's bar and stash it
in the corner and sit at the bar, feeling my railroad ticket, and have two hours to drink and wait.

90

The name of the place is Le Cigare.

Fournier the owner comes in, only 35, and right away gets on the phone going like this: "Allo, oui, cinque, yeh, quatre, yeh, deux, bon," bang the phone hook. I realize it's a bookie joint.

O then I tell them joyously "And who do you think is the best jockey today in America? Hah?"

As if they cared.

"Turcotte!" I yell triumphantly. "A Frenchman! Dint you see him win that Preakness?"

Preakness, Shmeakness, they never even heard of it, they've got the Grand Prix de Paris to worry about not to mention the Prix du Conseil Municipal and the Prix Gladiateur and the St. Cloud and Maisons Lafitte and Auteuil tracks, and Vincennes too, I gape to think what a big world this is that international horseplayers let alone pool players cant even get together.

But Fournier's real nice to me and says "We had a couple French Canadians in here last week, you shoulda been here, they left their cravats on the wall: see em? They had a guitar and sang *turlutus* and had a *big* time."

"Remember their names?"

"Nap—But you, American passport, Lebris de Kerouac you say, and came here to find news of your family, why you leaving Brest in a few hours?"

"Well,—now *you* tell me."

"Seems to me" (*"me semble"*) "if you made that much of an effort to come all the way out here, and all the trouble getting here, thru Paris and the libraries you say, now that you're here, it would be a shame if you didnt at least call up and go see *one* of the Lebris in this phone book—Look, there's dozens of em here. Lebris the pharmacist, Lebris the lawyer, Lebris the judge, Lebris the wholesaler, Lebris the restaurateur, Lebris the book dealer, Lebris the sea captain, Lebris the pediatrician—"

"Is there a Lebris who's a gynecologist who loves women's thighs" (*Ya tu un Lebris qu'est un gynecologiste qui aime les cuisses des femmes?*) yell I, and everybody in the bar, including Fournier's barmaid, and the old guy on the stool beside me, naturally, *laugh*.

"—Lebris—hey, no jokes—Lebris the banker, Lebris of the Tribunal, Lebris the mortician, Lebris the importer—"

"Call up Lebris the restaurateur and I'll give *my* cravat." And I take my blue knit rayon necktie off and hand it to him and open my collar like I'm at home. "I cant understand these French telephones," I add, and add to myself: ("But O you sure do" because I'm reminded of my great buddy in America who sits on the edge of his bed from first race to ninth race, butt in mouth, but not a big romantic smoking Humphrey Bogart butt, it's just an old Marlboro tip, brown and burnt-out from yesterday, and he's so fast on the phone he might bite flies if they dont get outa the way, as soon's he picks up the phone it's not even rung yet but somebody's talking to him: "Allo Tony? That'll be four, six, three, for a fin.")

Who ever thought that in my quest for ancestors I'd end up in a bookie joint in Brest, O Tony? brother of my friend?

Anyway Fournier does get on the phone, gets

Lebris the restaurateur, has me use my most elegant French getting meself invited, hangs up, holds up his hands, and says: "There, go see this Lebris."

"Where are the ancient Kerouacs?"

"Probably in Cornouialles country at Quimper, somewhere in Finistère south of here, he'll tell you. My name is Breton also, why get excited?"

"It's not *every* day."

"So *nu?*" (more or less). "Excuse me" and the phone rings. "And take back your necktie, it's a nice tie."

"Is Fournier a Breton name?"

"Why shore."

"What the hell," I yelled, "everybody's suddenly a Breton! Havet — LeMaire — Gibon — Fournier — Didier — Goulet — L'Évêsque — Noblet — Where's old Halmalo, and the old Marquis de Lantenac, and the little Prince of Kérouac, *Çiboire, j'pas capable trouvez ca*—" (*Çiborium*, I cant find that).

"Just like the horses?" says Fournier. "No! The lawyers in the little blue berets have changed all that. Go see Monsieur Lebris. And dont forget, if you come back to Brittany and Brest, come on over here with your friends, or your mother—or your cousins—But now the telephone is ringing, excuse me, Monsieur."

So I cut outa there carrying that suitcase down the Rue de Siam in broad daylight and it weighs a ton.

30.

NOW STARTS ANOTHER ADVENTURE. IT'S A MARVEL-
ous restaurant just like Johnny Nicholson's in
New York City, all marble-topped tables and ma-
hogany and statuary, but very small, and here,
instead of guys like Al and others rushing around
in tight pants serving table, are girls. But they
are the daughters and friends of the owner, Lebris. I come in and say where's Mr. Lebris, I been
invited. They say wait here and they go off and
check, upstairs. Finally it's okay and I carry my
suitcase up (feeling they didnt even believe me
in the first place, those gals) and I'm shown a bed-
room where lies a sharpnosed aristocrat in bed in
mid day with a huge bottle of cognac at his side,
plus I guess cigarettes, a comforter as big as
Queen Victoria on top of his blankets (a comforter, that is, I mean a six-by-six *pillow*), and his
blond doctor at the foot of the bed advising him

94

how to rest—"Sit down here" but even as that's
happening a *romancier de police* walks in, that is,
a writer of detective novels, wearing neat steel-
rimmed spectacles and himself as clean as the pin
o Heaven, with his charming wife—But then in
walks in poor Lebris' wife, a superb brunette
(mentioned to me by Fournier) and three *ravissan-
tes* (ravishing) girls who turn out to be one wed
and two unwed daughters—And there I am being
handed a cognac by Monsieur Lebris as he painstakingly raises himself from his heap of delicious
pillows (O Proust!) and says to me liltingly:

"You are Jean-Louis Lebris de Kérouac, you
said and they said on the phone?"

"Sans doute, Monsieur." I show him my passport which says: "John Louis Kerouac" because
you cant go around America and join the Merchant Marine and be called "Jean." But Jean is
the man's name for John, *Jeanne* is the woman's
name, but you cant tell that to your Bosun on the
S. S. Robert Treat Paine when the harbor pilot
calls on you to man the wheel through the mine
nets and says at your side "Two fifty one steady
as you go."

"Yes sir, two fifty one steady as I go."

"Two fifty, steady as you go."

"Two fifty, steady as I go."

"Two forty nine, steady, stead-y-y as you go"
and we go glidin right amongst them mine nets,
and into haven. (Norfolk 1944, after which I
jumped ship.) Why did the pilot pick old Keroach?
(Keroac'h, early spelling hassle among my uncles).
Because Keroach has a steady hand you buncha
rats who cant write let alone read books—

So my name on the passport is "John," and was once Shaun when O'Shea and I done Ryan in and Murphy laughed and all we done Ryan in, was a pub.

"And your name?" I ask.

"Ulysse Lebris."

Over the pillow comforter was the genealogical chart of his family, part of which is called Lebris de Loudéac, which he'd apparently called for preparatorily for my arrival. But he's just had a hernia operation, that's why he's in bed, and his doctor is concerned and telling him to do what should be done, and then leaves.

At first I wonder "Is he Jewish? pretending to be a French aristocrat?" because something about him looks Jewish at first, I mean the particular racial type you sometimes see, pure *skinny* Semitic, the serpentine forehead, or shall we say, aquiline, and that long nose, and funny hidden Devil's Horns where his baldness starts at the sides, and surely under that blanket he must have long thin feet (unlike my thick short fat peasant's feet) that he must waddle aside to aside *gazotsky* style, i.e., stuck out and walking on heels instead of front soles—And his foppish delightful airs, his Watteau fragrance, his Spinoza eye, his Seymour Glass (or Seymour Wyse) elegance tho I then realize I've never seen anybody who looked like that except at the end of a lance in another lifetime, a regular *blade* who took long coach trips from Brittany to Paris maybe with Abelard to just watch bustles bounce under chandeliers, had affairs in rare cemeteries, grew sick of the city and returned to his evenly distributed trees thru which

at least his mount knew how to canter, trot, gallop
or take off—A coupla stone walls between Com-
bourg and Champsecret, what matters it? A real
elegant—

Which I told him right off, still studying his
face to see if he was Jewish, but no, his nose was
as gleeful as a razor, his blue eyes languid, his
Devil's Horns out-and-out, his feet out of sight,
his French diction perfectly clear to anybody even
old Carl Adkins of West Virginia if he'd been
there, every word meant to be understood, Ah me,
to meet an old noble Breton, like tell that old
Gabriel de Montgomeri the joke is over—For a
man like this armies would form.

It's that old magic of the Breton noble and of
the Breton genius, of which Master Matthew Ar-
nold said: "A note of Celtic extraction, which
reveals some occult quality in a familiar object, or
tinges it, one knows not how, with 'the light that
never was on sea or land.'"

31.

KUDOS EVER, BUT OVER, WE BEGIN A LICK OF CON-
versation—(Again, dear Americans of the land
of my birth, in ratty French comparable in con-
text to the English they speak in Essex) :– Me:–
"Ah sieur, shite, one more cognac."

"'Ere you are, mighty." (A pun on "matey"
there and let me ask you but one more question,
reader:– Where else but in a book can you go back
and catch what you missed, and not only that but
savor it and keep it up and shove it? D'any Aussie
ever tell you that?)

I say: "But my, you are an elegant character,
hey what?"

No answer, just a bright glance.

I feel like a clod has to esplain himself. I gaze
on him. His head is turned parrotwise at the novelist and the ladies. I notice a glint of interest in
the novelist's eyes. Maybe he's a cop since he

writes police novels. I ask him across the pillows
if he knows Simenon? And has he read Dashiell
Hammett, Raymond Chandler and James M. Cain,
not to mention B. Traven?

I could better go into long serious controversies
with M. Ulysse Lebris did he read Nicholas Breton
of England, John Skelton of Cambridge, or the
ever-grand Henry Vaughan not to mention George
Herbert—and you could add, or John Taylor the
Water-Poet of the Thames?

Me and Ulysse cant even get a word in edgewise
thru our own thoughts.

32.

BUT I'M HOME, THERE'S NO DOUBT ABOUT IT, EXCEPT
if I were to want a strawberry, or loosen Alice's
shoetongue, old Herrick in his grave *and* Ulysse
Lebris would both yell at me to leave things alone,
and that's when I raw my wide pony and roll.

Well, Ulysse then turns to me bashfully and
just looks into my eyes briefly, and then away,
because he knows no conversation is possible when
every Lord and his blessed cat has an opinion on
everything.

But he looks and says "Come over and see my
genealogy" which I do, dutifully, I mean, I cant
see any more anyhow, but with my finger I trace
a hundred old names indeed branching out in
every direction, all Finistère and also Côtes du
Nord and Morbihan names.

Now think for a minute of these three names :–

(1) Behan
(2) Mahan
(3) Morbihan

Han? (for "Mor" only means "Sea" in Breton Celtic.)

I search blindly for that old Breton name Daoulas, of which "Duluoz" was a variation I invented just for fun in my writerly youth (to use as my name in my novels).

"Where is the record of your family?" snaps Ulysse.

"In the Rivistica Heraldica!" I yell, when I shoulda said "Rivista Araldica" which are Italian words meaning: "Heraldic Review."

He writes it down.

His daughter comes in again and says she's read some of my books, translated and published in Paris by that publisher who was out for lunch, and Ulysse is surprised. In fact his daughter wants my autograph. In fact I'm very Jerry Lewis himself in Heaven in Brittany in Israel getting high with Malachiah.

33.

ALL JOKING ASIDE, M. LEBRIS WAS, AND IS, YAIR,
an ace—I even went so far as to help myself, to
myself's own invitation (but with a polite (?) eh?)
to a third cognac, which at the time I thought had
mortified the *romancier de police* but he never
even glanced my way as tho he was studying
marks of my fingernails on the floor—(or lint)—

The fact of the matter is, (again that cliché, but
we need signposts), me and M. Lebris talked a
blue streak about Proust, de Montherlant, Chateaubriand, (where I told Lebris he had the same
nose), Saskatchewan, Mozart, and then we talked
of the futility of Surrealism, the loveliness of
loveliness, Mozart's flute, even Vivaldi's, by God
I even mentioned Sebastian del Piombo and how
he was even more languid than Raffaelc, and he
countered with the pleasures of a good comforter
(at which point I reminded him paranoiacally of

the Paraclete), and he went on, expounding 'pon
the glories of Armorica (ancient name of Brittany,
ar, "on," *mor*, "the sea,") and I then told him with
a dash of thought:– or hyphen:– *"C'est triste de
trouver que vous êtes malade, Monsieur Lebris"*
(pronounced Lebriss), "It's sad to find that you're
ill, Monsieur Lebris, but joyous to find that you're
encircled by your lovers, truly, in whose company
I should always want to be found."

This is all in fancy French and he answered
"That's well put, and with eloquence *and* elegance,
in a manner not always understood nowadays"
(and here we sorta winked at each other as we
realized we were going to start a routine of talking like two overblown mayors or archbishops,
just for fun and to test my formal French), "and
it doesnt disturb me to say, in front of my family
and my friends, that you are the equal of the idol
who has given you your inspiration" (*que vous
êtes l'égale de l'idole qui vous à donnez votre inspiration*), "if that thought is any comfort to you,
you who, doubtless, have no need of comfort among
those who wait upon you."

Picking up: "But, *certes*, Monsieur, your words,
like the flowered barbs of Henry Fifth of England
addressed to the poor little French princess, and
right in front of his, Oh me, *her* chaperone, not
as if to cut but as the Greeks say, the sponge of
vinegar in the mouth was not a cruelty but (again,
as we know on the Mediterranean sea) a shot that
kills the thirst."

"Well of course, expressed that way, I shall
have no more words, but, in my feebleness to understand the extent of my vulgarities, but that is

to say supported by your faith in my undignified
efforts, the dignity of our exchange of words is
understood surely by the cherubs, but that's not
enough, *dignity* is such an exe-crable word, and
now, before—but no I havent lost the line of my
ideas, Monsieur Kerouac, he, in his excellence,
and that excellence which makes me forget all, the
family, the house, the establishment, in any case:—
a sponge of vinegar *kills* the thirst?"

"Say the Greeks. And, if I could continue to explain everything that I know, your ears would lose
the otiose air they wear now—You have, dont in-
terrupt me, listen—"

"Otiose! A word for the Chief Inspector Char-
lot, dear Henri!"

The French detective story writer's not interested in my otiose, or my odious nuther, but I'm
trying to give you a stylish reproduction of how
we talked and what was going on.

I sure hated to leave that sweet bedside.

Besides, lots of brandy there, as tho I couldnt
go out and buy my own.

When I told him the motto of my ancestral family, *"Aimer, Travailler et Souffrir"* (Love, Work
and Suffer) he said: "I like the *Love* part, as for
Work it gave me hernia, and Suffer you see me
now."

Goodbye, Cousin!

P.S. (And the shield was: "Blue with gold
stripes accompanied by three silver nails.")

In sum: In "Armorial Général de J. B. Riestap,
Supplement par V. H. Rolland: LEBRIS DE
KEROACK—Canada, originaire de Bretagne.
D'azur au chevron d'or accompagné de 3 clous

d'argent. D :– AIMER, TRAVAILLER ET SOUF-
FRIR. RIVISTA ARALDICA, IV, 240."

And old Lebris de Loudéac he shall certainly see
Lebris de Kéroack again, unless one of us, or both
of us, die—Which I remind my readers goes back
to : Why change your name unless you're ashamed
of something.

34.

BUT I GOT SO FASCINATED BY OLD DE LOUDÉAC, AND not one taxi outside on Rue de Siam, I had to hurry with that 70 pound suitcase in my paw, switching it from paw to paw, and missed my train to Paris by, count it, three minutes.

And I had to wait eight hours till eleven in the cafes around the station—I told the yard switchmen: "You mean to tell me I missed that Paris train by *three* minutes? What are you Bretons tryna do, *keep* me here?" I went over to the deadend blocks and pressed against the oiled cylinder to see if it would give and it did so now at least I could write a letter (that'll be the day) back to Southern Pacific railroad brakemen now train masters and oldheads that in France they couple different, which I s'pose sounds like a dirty postcard, but it's true, but dingblast it I've lost ten pounds running from Ulysse Lebris' restaurant to the station (one mile) with that bag, alright, shove it, I'll store the bag in baggage and drink for eight hours—

But, as I unpin my little McCrory suitcase (Monkey Ward it actually was) key, I realize I'm too drunk and mad to open the lock (I'm looking for my tranquilizers which you must admit I need by now), in the suitcase, the key is pinned as according to my mother's instructions to my clothes —For a full twenty minutes I kneel there in the baggage station of Brest Brittany trying to make the little key open the snaplock, cheap suitcase anyhow, finally in a Breton rage I yell " *O u v r e d o n c   m a u d i t* !" (OPEN UP DAMN YOU!!) and break the lock—I hear laughter—I hear someone say: "Le roi Kerouac" (the king Kerouac). I'd heard that from the wrong mouths in America. I take off the blue knit rayon necktie and, after taking out a pill or two, and an odd flask of cognac, I press down on the suitcase with the broken lock (one of em broken) and I wrap the necktie around, make one full twist tight, pull tight, and then, grabbing one end of the necktie in my teeth and pulling whilst holding the knot down with middle (or woolie) finger, I endeavor to bring the other end of the necktie around the taut toothpulled end, loop it in, steady as you go, then lower my great grinning teeth to the suitcase of all Brittany, till I'm kissing it, and *bang!,* mouth pulls one way, hand the other, and that thing is tied tighter than a tied-ass mother's everloving son, or son of a bitch, *one.*

And I dump it in baggage and get my baggage ticket.

Spend most of the time talking to big corpulent
Breton cabdrivers, what I learned in Brittany is
"Dont be afraid to be big, fat, be yourself if you're
big and fat." Those big fat sonumgun Bretons
waddle around as tho the last whore of summer
war lookin for her first lay. You cant drive a spike
with a tack hammer, say the Polocks, well at least
said Stanley Twardowicz which is another country I've never seen. You can drive a *nail*, but not
a spike.

So I hang around doodling about, for awhile I
sigh to eye clover on top of a cliff where I actually
could go take a five-hour nap except a lot of little
cheap faggots or poets are watching every move
I make, it's broad afternoon, how can I go lie
down in the tall grass if some Seraglio learns
about my remaining $100 on my dear sweet arse?

I'm telling you, I'm getting so suspicious of
men, and now less of women, it would make Diana
weep, or cough laughing, *one*.

I was really afraid of falling asleep in those
weeds, unless nobody saw me sneak into them, to
my trapdoor at last, but alas, the Algerians'd
found a new home, not to mention Bodhidharma
and his boys walking over water from Chaldea
(and walking on water wasnt built in a day.)

Why perdure the reader's might? The train
came at eleven and I got on the first firstclass
coach and got into the first compartment and was
alone and put my feet up on the opposite seat as
the train rolled out and I heard somebody say to
another guy:—

"*Le roi n'est pas amusez.*" (The king is not

amused.) ("You frigging A!" I shoulda yelled out
the window.)

And a sign said:- "Dont throw anything out
the window" and I yelled *"J'n'ai rien à jeter en
dehors du chaussi, ainque ma tête!"* (I got nothing to throw out the window, only my head). My
bag was with me—I heard from the other car,
"Ça c'est un Kérouac," (Now that's a Kerouac)—
I dont even think I was hearing right, but dont be
too sure, about not only Brittany but a land of
Druids and Witchcraft and Warlocks and Féeries
—(not Lebris)—

Let me just brief you on the last happening that
I remember in Brest:- afraid to sleep in those
weeds, which were not only at edges of cliffs in
full sight of people's third story windows but as
I say in full view of wandering punks, I simply in
despair sat with the cabdrivers at the cab stand,
me on the stone wall—All of a sudden a ferocious
vocal fight broke out between a corpulent blue
eyed Breton cabdriver and a thin mustachio'd
Spanish or I guess Algerian or maybe Provençal
cabdriver, to hear them, their "Come on, if you
wanta start something with me *start*" (the Breton) and the younger mustachio "Rrrratratra-
tra!" (some fight about positions in the cab stand,
and there I was a few hours ago couldnt find a cab
on Main Street)—I was sitting at this point on
the stone curb watching the progress of a lil ole
caterpillar in whose fate I was of course particu-
larly fishponded, and I said to the first cab in line
at the cab stand:

"In the first place goddamit, *cruise,* cruise thru

town for fares, dont hang around this dead railroad station, there might be an Évêsque wants a ride after a sudden visit to a donor of the church—"

"Well, it's the union" etc.

I said "See those two son of a bitches fighting over there, I dont like him."

No answer.

"I dont like the one who's not the Breton—not the old one, the *young* one."

The cabdriver looks away at a new development in front of the railroad station, which is, a young vesperish mother toting an infant in her arms and a non-Breton hoodlum on a motorcycle coming to bring a telegram almost knocking her down, but at least scaring the heart out of her.

"That," I say to my Breton Brother, "is a *voyou*" (hoodlum)—"Why did he do it to that lady and her child?"

"To attract all our attention," he practically leered. He added: "I have a wife and kids on the hill, across the bay you see there, with the boats . . ."

"Hoodlums are what gave Hitler his start."

"I'm first in line in this cab stand, let them fight and be hoodlums all they want—When the time comes, the time comes."

"*Bueno*," I said like a Spanish pirate of St. Malo, "*Garde a campagne*." (Guard your countryside).

He didnt even have to answer, that big corpulent 220-pound Breton, first in line on the cab stand, his eyes himself would sclowber scubaduba

or anything else they wanta throw at 'im, and O
most bullshit Jack, the people are not asleep.

And when I say "the people" I dont mean that
created-in-the-textbook mass first called at me at
Columbia College as "Proletariat," and not now
called at me as "Unemployed Disenchanted Ghetto-
Dwelling Misfits," or in England as "Mods and
Rods," I say, the People are first, second, third,
fourth, fifth, sixth, seventh, eighth, ninth, tenth,
eleventh and twelfth in the cabstand line and if
you try to bug them, you may find yourself with a
blade of grass in your bladder, which cuts finest.

35.

THE CONDUCTOR SEES ME WITH MY FEET ON THE
other seat and yells *"Les pieds a terre!"* (Feet on
the ground!) My dreams of being an actual descendant of the Princes of Brittany are shattered
also by the old French hoghead blowing at the
crossing whatever they blow at French crossings,
and of course shattered also by that conductor's
enjoinder, but then I look up at the plaque over
the seat where my feet had been:–

*"This seat reserved for those wounded in the
service of France."*

So I ups and goes to the compartment next, and
the conductor looks in to collect my ticket and I
say "I didnt see that sign."

He says "That's awright, but take your shoes
off."

This King will ride second fiddle to anyone so
long's he can blow like my Lord.

36.

AND ALL NIGHT ALONG, ALONE IN AN OLD PASSENGER
coach, Oh Anna Karenina, O Myshkin, O Rogo-
zhin, I ride back St. Brieuc, Rennes, got my
brandy, and there's Chartres at dawn—
 Arriving in Paris in the morning.
 By this time, from the cold of Bretagne, I got
big flannel shirt on now, with scarf inside collar,
no shave, pack silly hat away into suitcase, close
it again with teeth and now, with my Air France
return trip ticket to Tampa Florida I'se ready as
the fattest ribs in old Winn Dixie, dearest God.

37.

IN THE MIDDLE OF THE NIGHT, BY THE WAY, AS I
marveled at the s's of darkness and light, a mad
eager man of 28 got on the train with an 11-year-
old girl and escorted her gainingly to the compartment of the wounded, where I could hear him
yelling for hours till she gave him the fish eye and
fell asleep on her own seat alone—*La Muse de la
Départment* and *Le Provinçial à Paris* missed by
a coupla years, O Balzac, O in fact Nabokov . . .
(The Poetess of the Provinces and the Hick in
Paris.) (Whattayou expect with the Prince of
Brittany a compartment away?)

38.

So here we are in Paris. All's over. From now on I'm finished with any and all forms of Paris life. Carrying my suitcase I'm accosted at the gates by a cab-hawk. "I wanta go to Orly" I say.

"Come on!"

"But first I need a beer and a cognac across the street!"

"Sorry no time!" and he turns to other customers calling and I realize I might as well get on my horse if I'm gonna be home tonight Sunday night in Florida so I say:—

"Okay. *Bon, allons.*"

He grabs my bag and lugs it to a waiting cab on the misting sidewalk. A thin-mustached Parisian cabdriver is packing in two ladies with a babe in arms in the back of his hack and meanwhile socking in their luggage in the compartment out back. My fella socks my bag in, asks for 3 or 5 francs,

I fergit. I look at the cabdriver as if to say "In front?" and he says with head "Yeah."

I say to myself "Another thin nosed sonumbitch in *Paris-est-Pourri* shit, he wouldnt care if you roasted your grandmother over coals long as he could get her earrings and maybe gold teeth."

In the front seat of the little sports taxi I search vainly for an ashtray at my righthand front door. He whips out a weird ashtray arrangement beneath the dashboard, with a smile. He then turns to the ladies in back as he zips through that six-intersection place right outside Toulouse-Lautrec's loose too-much and pipes:—

"Darling little child! How old is she?"

"Oh, seven months."

"How many others you have."

"Two."

"And that's your, eh, Mother."

"No my aunt."

"I thought so, of course, she doesn't look like you, of course with my uncanny whatnots—In any case a delightful child, a mother we need speak no further, *of*, and an aunt make all Auvergne rejoice!"

"How did you know we were Auvergnois?!"

"Instinct, instinct, since I am! How are you there, feller, where going?"

"Me?" I say with dismal Breton breath. "To Florida" (*à Floride*).

"Ah it must be beautiful there! And you, my dear aunt, how many children did you have?"

"Oh—seven."

"Tsk, tsk, almost too much. And is the little one giving you any trouble?"

"No—not a mite."

"Well there you have it. All's well, really,"
swinging in a wide 70-m.p.h.-arc around the Sainte
Chapelle where as I said before the piece of the
True Cross is kept and was put there by St. Louis
of France, King Louis 9th, and I said:-

"Is *that* la Sainte Chapelle? I meant to see it."

"Ladies," he says to the back seat, "you're going
where? Oh yes, Gare St. Lazare, yes, here we are
—Just another minute"—Zip—

"There we are" and he leaps out as I sit there
dumbfounded and blagdenfasted and hauls out
their suitcases, whistles for a boy, has them
whisked off baby and all, and leaps back into the
cab alone with me saying: "Orly was it?"

"Aye, *mais*, but, Monsieur, a glassa beer for the
road."

"Bah—it'll take me ten minutes."

"Ten minutes is too long."

He looks at me seriously.

"Well, I can stop off at a cafe on the way where
I can double park and you throw it down real fast
'cause I'm working this Sunday morning, ah,
Life."

"You have one with me."

Zip

"Here it is. Out."

We jump out, run into this cafe thru the now-
rain, and duck up to the bar and order two beers.
I tell him:-

"If you're in a real hurry I'll show you how to
chukalug a beer down!"

"No necessity," he says sadly, "we have a minute."

He suddenly reminds me of Fournier the bookie in Brest.

He tells me his name, of Auvergne, I mine, of Brittany.

At the spot instant when I know he's ready to fly I open my gullet and let a halfbottle of beer fall down a hole, a trick I learned in Phi Gamma Delta fraternity now I see for no small reason (holding up kegs at dawn, and with no pledge cap because I refused it and besides I was on the football team), and in the cab we jump like bankrobbers and ZAM! we're going 90 in the rain slick highway to Orly, he tells me how many kilometers fast he's going, I look out the window and figure it's our cruising speed to the next bar in Texas.

We discuss politics, assassinations, marriages, celebrities, and when we get to Orly he hauls my bag out the back and I pay him and he jumps right back in and says (in French) : "Not to repeat myself, me man, but today Sunday I'm working to support my wife and kids—And I heard what you told me about families in Quebec that had kids by the twenties and twenty-fives, that's too much, that is—Me I've only got two—But, work, yes, yowsah, this and that, or as you say Monsieur thissa and thatta, in any case, thanks, be of good heart, I'm going."

"Adieu, Monsieur Raymond Baillet," I say.

The Satori taxidriver of page one.

When God says "I Am Lived," we'll have forgotten what all the parting was about.

Pic

DEDICATED TO DR. DANNY DESOLE

CONTENTS

1. ME AND GRANDPA

AIN'T NEVER NOBODY LOVED ME like I love myself,
cept my mother and she's dead. (My grandpa, he's
so old he can remember a hunnerd years back but
what happened last week and the day before, he
don't know.) My pa gone away so long ago ain't
nobody remember what his face like. My brother,
ever' Sunday afternoon in his new suit in front of
the house, out on that old road, and grandpa and
me just set on the porch rockin and talkin, but my
brother paid it no mind and one day he was gone
and ain't never been back.

Grandpa, when we was alone, said he'd ten' the
pigs and I go mend the fence yonder, and said, "I
seed the Lawd come thu that fence a hunnerd
years ago and He shall come again." My Aunt
Gastonia come by buttin and puffin said that it

was all right, she believed it too, she'd seen the Lord more times than they could ever count, and hallelujahed and hallelujahed, said "While's all this the Gospel word and true, little Pictorial Review Jackson" (that's me) "must go to school to learn and read and write," and grandpa looked at her plum in the eye like if'n to spit tobacco juice in it, and answered, "Thass awright wif me," jess like that, "but that ain't the Lawd's school he's goin' to and he shall never mend his fences."

So I went to school, and came on home from school the afternoon after it and seed nobody would ever know where I come from, if what they called it was North Carolina. It didn't feel like no North Carolina to me. They said I was the darkest, blackest boy ever come to that school. I always knowed *that*, cause I seen white boys come by my house, and I seed pink boys, and I seed blue boys, and I seed green boys, and I seed orange boys, then black, but never seed one so black as me.

Well, I gave this no never mind, and 'joyed myself and made some purty pies when I was awful little till I seed it rully did smell awful bad; and all that, and grandpa a-grinnin from the porch, and smokin his old green pipe. One day two white boys came by seed me and said I was verily black as nigger chiles go. Well, I said that I knowed *that* indeedy. They said they seed I was too small for what they was about, which I now forget, and I said it was a mighty fine frog peekin from his hand.

He said it was no frog, but a TOAD, and said
TOAD like to make me jump a hunnerd miles
high, he said it so plain and loud, and they ske-
daddled over the hill back of my grandpa's prop-
erty. So I knew they was a North Carolina, and
they was a *toad*, and I dreamed of it 'at night.

On the crossroads Mr. Dunaston let me and old
hound dog sit on the steps of his store ever' blessed
evenin and I heard the purty singin on the radio
just as *plain*, and just as *good*, and learned me two,
th'ee, seben songs and sing them. Here come Mr.
Otis one time in his big old au-to, bought me two
bottles Dr. Pepper, en I took one home to
grandpa: *he* said Mr. Otis was a mighty fine man
and he knowed his pappy and his pappy's pappy
clear back a hunnerd years, and they was good
folks. Well, I knowed *that:* and we 'greed, and
'greed Dr. Pepper allus did make a spankin' good
fizzle for folkses' moufs. Y'all can tell how I 'joyed
myself then.

Well here's all where it was laid out. My grandpa's house, it was all lean-down and 'bout to
break, made of sawed planks sawed when they was
new from the woods and here they was all wore
out like poor dead stumplewood and heavin out in
the middle. The roof was like to slip offen its
hinges and fall on my grandpa's head. He make it
no mind and set there, rockin. The inside of the
house was clean like a ear of old dry corn, and jess
as crinkly and dead and good for me barefoot as

y'all seed if you tried it. Grandpa and me sleep in
the big old tinkle-bed and gots room all over, it's
so big. Hound dog sleep in the door. Never did
close that door till winter come. I cut the wood,
grandpa light it into stove. Set there eatin peas and
greens and sassmeat and here's a BIG spoon and
eat a lot till my belly's all out—when they was a
lot. Well, Aunt Gastonia, she bring us food, here,
there, last week, next month. Bring us sassmeat,
storebread, streak-a-lean. Grandpa grow the peas
in the field, and grow the corn field by the fence,
and then we fetched the pigs what we grind outen
our moufs cause we no cain't chaw it. Hound dog,
eat too. House set in the middle of the field. Yonder's the road, sand road all wore hard and pebbly,
and the mules comin by and every now'n then a
big au-to thrown up a fine cloud a mile high and
me smellin it ever'where and sayin to myself,
"Now what fo the Lawd don't make hisself mo
clean?" Then I snups out me nose, Shah! Well,
over yonder is Mr. Dunaston's store at the crossroads, and then the piney woods wif old crow settin ever' mornin on the branch jess cra-a-cra-a-kin,
to beat hisself, and me say cra-cra-cra-cra jess like
he do, and I gotsa laugh, ever' morning, hee hee
hee, it tickle me so. Then yonder th' other way is
Mr. Dunaston's brother's tobacco, n'a big, big
house Mr. Otis live in, and Miz Bell's house in the
middler the field and Miz Bell she like to be as old
as grandpa and smoke the pipe jess like he do.

Well, she like me. Ever' night ever'body sleep in
this house and that house and ever' house, and the
only thing you can hear is a old owl—hooo! hooo!
—out in the woods, and yek! yek! yek! all the bats,
and the yowlin hound dogs, 'n the cricket-bugs a-
creekin' in the dark. Then there's the choo-choo
out by TOWN, y'know. Only thing you can't hear
is a old spider spinnin his cobweb. I go on in the
shanty and break a cobweb—after I wipe myself
that old spider, he make 'nother cobweb for me.
Up yonder in the sky, they's a hunnerd motion
stars and here on the ground hit's as *wet,* as like
to'd rain. I gets me in the bed and grandpa say,
"Boy, keep your big wet feet from me!" but in a little bitty while my feets is dry and I'se tucked in
good. Then I see the stars thu the window n' I
sleep good.

Y'all can tell how I 'joyed myself then?

2. WHAT HAPPENED

PO GRANDPA, he never get up one mornin, and ever'body come over from Aunt Gastonia's and said he was 'bout to die of misery. On grandpa's pillow I laid my head down and HE tell me it ain't so. And he yell to the Lord to git ever'body outen the house except the good hound dog. Hound dog set a-whinin' under the bed and lick grandpa in the hand. Aunt Gastonia shoo him out. "Hound dog, shoo!" Aunt Gastonia wash my face at the pump. Aunt Gastonia, she put the rag in my ear and stop up the ear and take her finger and turn and turn till I'se 'bout to die. Well, I cry. Grandpa cry too. Aunt Gastonia's son, he run and he run down that road and pooty soon, here come Aunt Gastonia's son run and run back up the road and zip-zip I never seed nobody run s'fast. Then here come Mr.

Otis in his big old au-to and pull up right in front
of the house. Well, he was a pow'ful tall man with
yaller hair, you know, and *he* 'membered me, and
says, "Well there, what's to become of you, li'l
boy?"

Then he take grandpa by the hand, and roll up
his eyeballs, and fish in the black satchel fo a thing
he listen with, and listen, and ever'body else lean
close and listen, and Aunt Gastonia slap her son
away, and Mr. Otis 'bout to tap grandpa with one
hand under th' other on grandpa's chest, when him
and grandpa gits they eyes fixed on theirselves all
sow'ful and Mr. Otis stop what he doing. "Ah, old
man," Mr. Otis say to grandpa, "and how have
you been?" And grandpa show his yaller teeth in a
grin and he say, and he cackle, "Yonder's the pipe,
hit's a pow'ful smokin-pipe," and wink at Mr. Otis.
Nobody know what he talk like that fo, but Mr.
Otis *he* know and grandpa he laugh so much he
jess shake like the tree when the possum climb up
in it. Mr. Otis says "Where?" and grandpa point to
the shelf, still a-cacklin and 'joyin Mr. Otis so.
Well, he sho liked Mr. Otis ever so much. Up yonder on the shelf so high I never seed it, Mr. Otis
fetched a pipe they was talkin about. It was made
outen corncob and it was the biggenest best pipe
grandpa made. Mr. Otis, he look at it so sow'ful I
never seed that man so. He say "Five years," and
that's all he say, 'case that was the last time he seed
grandpa, and grandpa knowed it.

After a bit, grandpa fell asleep, and ever'body stand aroun talkin till I cain't see how anybody can sleep, and here's what they said. They said grandpa was mighty sick and would die for sho, and me, li'l Pic, well what was they t'do with me? Oh, it was a tar'ble lot of cryin they was doin Aunt Gastonia and her friend Miz Jones, 'case they loved grandpa like I do, the son *he* cry too, and all the little bitty chiles that come in the door from the road t'see. Hound dog, he whined outdoor t'come in. Mr. Otis, he told ever'body t'stop worryin' their minds so, mebbe grandpa be all right soon, but he'd no fo-sure about it, so he's gwine see about sendin grandpa to the *hospital,* and there he be all right. Ever'body 'gree this is what to do and's grateful to Mr. Otis, 'case he pay with all his money t'see grandpa try to get good again. "The boy," he say, t'Aunt Gastonia, "you sure your husband and your father see eye to eye with you 'bout keepin that boy?" and she say, "The Lord shall bring mercy unto them." And Mr. Otis say, "Well, I don't reckon it will be so but you take good care of him, hear, and let me know if ever'thing's all right." Lordy, I cry when I heard ever'thing and ever'body talkin so. Oh Lordy, I cry when they takes poor grandpa and carry him to the car like some old sick run-over hound dog and lay him in the back seat, and carry him off to the *hospital.* I cry, Aunt Gastonia she close grandpa's door, and *he* never close it, never did once close it for a hunnerd years. The tar'ble fear make me sick and like to drop on the ground and dig me a hole and cry in it, n'hide, 'case I never seen anything but this house and grandpa all my born days, and here they come draggin me away from th' empty house and my grandpa's done died on me and can't help hisself dyin. Oh Lord, and I remember what he say 'bout the fence and the Lord, and 'bout Mr. Otis and 'bout my big wet feet, and remember him so awful recent and him s'far gone, I cry, and shame ever'body.

3. AUNT GASTONIA'S HOUSE

WELL, THEY TAKES ME DOWN THE ROAD to Aunt
Gastonia's house, and it's a big old busted house
'case they's eleben, twell folks livin there, from
down the littlest baby-chile up to old Grandpa
Jelkey 'at sits inside the house all old and blind. It
ain't like grandpa's house no way. Is all them windows roundabout and a big brick chimbley, and
the porch, it go clean around the house and chairs
on it, and watermelon rinds and sand on the
boards so's a body can't roll hisself without. My, I
never seed such many flies in all my born days like
I seed in that house. No, I don't wantsa stay here.
Trees in the barnyard, and cherry tree, and the
good swing, but they's six, seben chiles all squeal-
in and squawkin and the pigs is not so good as
grandpa's pigs never nohow. I never seed nothin so

134

tedious. No, I don't wantsa stay here. Gots no place to sleep at night exceptin in one bed with th'ee, fo boys, and I can't sleep with they elbows in my face.

Grandpa Jelkey, that man scare me 'case he say "Bring that boy here," and they brings me, and he take a holt of me by th' arms and look at me with one great big yaller eye but don't aim it right, poor thing, and look clear over my head and can't see nothing. Th' other eye, it ain't there no more, th' eyeball sunk inside his head. He got no eyes, that old man. He holt me tight and hurt me, and he say, "This here is the boy. Well, I ain't gots to touch the boy more'n one time a day." Aunt Gastonia, she run up and pull me off. "Why you wantsa curse that boy when y'already cursed ever'body seven times? It ain't his fault what his father done to your eyes, he's jess a chile." And Grandpa Jelkey, he shout up "I'se gwine touch him seben times afore he dies, ain't nobody stop me." "You ain't neither," Aunt Gastonia shout up, and Uncle Sim that's Aunt Gastonia's husband he gotsa take Aunt Gastonia outdoor, and me, I gotsa run and hide in the barnyard, 'case I'se sho scared Grandpa Jelkey reach out and catch me again. Nos'r, I don't like Aunt Gastonia's house, no.

Serpentine Grandpa Jelkey sit in the corner and eat offen his knee and ever'body else eat 'round the table-top, and Grandpa Jelkey hear ever'body talkin, and say "Is that you, boy?" and mean me. I hide b'hind Aunt Gastonia. "Come on stand by me, boy, so's I can touch you twicet. T'won't leave me none but four, and then you pays the curse." "Never pay no mind whad he say," Aunt Gastonia say to me. Uncle Sim he don't say nothin, and he never *look* at me neither, and I'se so scared and so sickly, well, I don't expect I'd a-lived in Aunt Gastonia's house long but t'go die in the woods and being so lowly and blue. Aunt Gastonia say I gits sick and lose eleben pounds, I'se so awful and feeble and lain in the dust all day. "What for you wantsa cry in the dirt, chile," say to me, "and git all that mud on your face like that?" She gotsa wipe the mud. Aunt Gastonia, it wasn't ever her, it was Grandpa Jelkey, and Uncle Simeon, and all the chiles th'ow sand at me. And ain't *nobody* take me see grandpa in the hospital. "Oh Lord, I gotsa stop cryin so."

Grandpa Jelkey, he reach out the window and cotch me and hurt me so I'se fall down dead, and he yell, and he whoop, and he say, "Now I'se cotch the boy and now I done touch him twicet!"—Then he say, then he say, "Th'ee!—fo!—" and Aunt Gastonia she yank me away s'hard I fall in the ground. "I done seed the sign, when I reach out to cotch him," Grandpa Jelkey yell, "and ain't but th'ee left now." Aunt Gastonia bust out cryin and fall on the bed and thrash hesself and don't know what and all the chiles run down the road t'git Uncle Sim what's in the field with the mule, and he

come runnin to the road. Lordy, then that old
Grandpa Jelkey come out on the porch lookin f'me
and spread his arms, f'me, and he come right
straight t'where I is standin like he was not blind
nohow, but then he stumble over the chair and
yowl out, fall down and hurt hisself. Ever'body say
Oh! Uncle Sim pick up th' old man and carry him
in the house and put him on the bed, and th' old
man gaspin. Uncle Simeon, he told cousin take me
outdoor, so me and cousin go stand outdoor, and
hear Uncle Sim and Aunt Gastonia a-yellin at
each other.

"What fo you wantsa keep that boy in this house
what has the curse laid on him, fool woman?"
Uncle Sim yell. And Aunt Gastonia, she pray and
she pray, "Oh Lord, he jess a chile, he ain't done a
thing t'nobody, what for the Lord bring shame and
destruction on the head of a innocent lamb, and a
leastest chile." "I ain't got nothin to do with what
the Lord decide," yell Uncle Sim. Aunt Gastonia
say "Lord God, his blood is my blood, and my sister's blood is my blood, Oh Lord, dear Jesus, save
us from sin, save my husband from sin, save my fa-
ther-'n-law from sin, save my chillun from sin, and
Lord, dear Lord, save ME, Gastonia Jelkey, from
sin." Uncle Sim, he come out on the porch and
give the blackenest look, and walk away, 'case
Aunt Gastonia she pray all night now, and *he*
don't got nothing to say. Grandpa Jelkey, he fall
asleep.

Well cousin older'n me take me down the road
and show me TOWN out yonder, 'case he knowed
I'se so forlorn. He say, "Tonight Satty night, ever-
'body git drunk and go to TOWN yonder and they
rocks, thass what they do, yas'r." I say, "What you
mean *rocks?*" He say, "Boy, they gots jumpin-
music and jamboree-singin and dancin all that
truck. Yas'r, I seed it Satty night, had some barbe-
cue pig and daddy he drink the bottle down like
'is"—and he throw his big head back, cousin, and
he have the biggenest head, y'know, and show me,
and say—"WHooee!" Then he jump around a-
holtin hisself by the arms t'show me, and he say,
"This here dancin. B'you cain't go to no jamboree
'case you gotsa curse on you." So me'n cousin go
down the road a bit, and they's all the lights of
TOWN I ain't never seed before, and we sits up in
the apple tree and sees all that. But I is so low-
down it don't make no neither much to me. Lordy,
what's I care about all that old town?

Well, cousin go thisaway and I go thataway, and
I traipse back up the woods and down the hill to
Mr. Dunaston's store, and hear me some radio
singin again. Then, you bet, I go way down that
road t'grandpa's house. It's all so still, s'empty,
well, ain't nobody know it but I is 'bout to die and
go to my death in the ground. Old hound dog
yowlin at grandpa's door, but *he* ain't livin there,
and I ain't livin there neither, ain't nobody livin

'bout it, and he yowl his soul.

Well, grandpa seed the Lord come thu the fence a hunnerd years ago, and now he gotsa die in the hospital and never get t'see no fence nor nothin no more. I ask to th' Lord, "What for the Lord do it to po grandpa?"

I cain't remember no more 'bout Aunt Gastonia's house and ever'thing done happened there.

4. BROTHER COME TO FETCH ME

A BOY LIKE ME AIN'T GOT NO PLACE TO SLEEP lessen he stay where he's at, and I sho didn't wantsa stay at Aunt Gastonia's no more, but jess ain't was nowhere for me to sleep but that po woman's house, so I traipse back thu the black woods, yes'r and there she is, Aunt Gastonia, waitin up f'me with the oil lamp in the kitchen. "Sleep, my chile," she say to me, and so kindly I'se like to fall and sleep on her knee, like I done on my mother's knee when I'se a little bitty chile, before she got die. "Aunt Gastonia take care of you no matter what," she say, and stroke m'head, and I fall asleep.

Well, I'se sick in the bed for two, th'ee, seben days and it rain and rain all the time and Aunt Gastonia feed me grits and sugar and heat up collard greens for me. Grandpa Jelkey, he sit on the

140

other side of the house and say "Bring that boy to
me," but ain't nobody bring me to him nor tell him
where I is, and Aunt Gastonia tell ever'body to
shush. Grandpa Jelkey cotch cousin thu the window like he done me, and he say, "Nope, I reckon
this ain't the boy." And cousin he howl like I did.

I sleep two days, and don't wake up none but for
to sleep again, and Aunt Gastonia she send cousin
to fetch Mr. Otis, but Mr. Otis he gone up
NORTH. "Where he gone up NORTH?" she say
to cousin, and cousin say, "Why he jess gone up
NORTH." "What part the NORTH he gone up
there?" and cousin say, "Why, he's gone up to
NORTH VIRGINIA." Aunt Gastonia, she bow
her po head down and don't know whatsa do.

So Mr. Otis is gone, and Aunt Gastonia pray for
me, and bring Miz Jones to pray for me too.

Uncle Sim, he look at me once, and he say to
Aunt Gastonia, "That boy's 'bout to folly his
grandaddy I reckon," and she look up to the roof
and say, "Amen, the world ain't fit for no such a
lamb, Jesus save his soul." "Well," say Uncle Sim,
"I don't guess it's but one less mouf t'feed," and
she shriek "Oh Jehovah guide my man from sinful
ways." "Shush your mouf, woman, this man ain't
got no time for sinful ways and he ain't a-gonna
get no new stove this winter neither, 'case that tobacco patch been cursed, hear, the bugs done
started eatin leaves since that boy been here." And
he stomp out the door.

Well, thass the longest talk I ever hear that man make.

I lay in the bed one Satty mornin, and W H O O P! they's ever'body yellin and talkin outdoor, and carryin on so loud I try to see and stretch my head way out but cain't see nothin. They all comes traipsin up the porch. Well I pull my head back 'case I'se sick. Well, who do you guess come in that door, and all the chillun grinnin behind?

If it ain't my brother, dog my cats, and he change so much since he go away from me and grandpa, I cain't for sure say *who* that man is standin in the door, 'case he gots a little bitty round hat on his head with a little bitty button on top of it, and hairs a-hangin from his chin p'culiar, and he all thin, and lean, and all drew-out tall, and sorry-lookin too. He laugh and laugh when he see me, and come over to the bed for t'catch me, and look at me in th'eye. "Here he is," he say, and it ain't nobody he talk it to, 'case he say it to hisself, and smile, and me, I'se so s'prised I don't say nothin. Well, y'know, I'se so s'prised it make me sit up in the bed.

All the chillun is grinnin, but Aunt Gastonia she trouble and fuss hesself, poor soul, and she keep lookin over her shoulder for fear Uncle Sim come up the road, 'case he don't like my brother neither, I don't reckon. "Looky here John, where you been and what's you come here for?" she say to my brother, and he say "Hey now" and jump up and

do the most comical shufflin 'bout the house I ever
seed, and I laugh, and all the chillun laugh with
me, and Grandpa Jelkey, he rare up and say,
"What fo ever'body laugh?"

"I come here to fetch Mister Pic, ma'm, and
bring him on my *magic carpet* up NORTH to
NEW YORK CITY, your grace," he say, and do
the most comical bow-down and fetch off his comical hat and show ever'body his head. The chiles
and me, we gotsa laugh again and you ain't never
seed such 'joyin and laughin. "Who that talkin?"
Grandpa Jelkey say, and he say "Why-all's them
chillun laugh so?" But ain't nobody tell him.

"How come you here?" Aunt Gastonia ask my
brother, and he tuck his hat under his arm and say,
"Why, for to get my brother, that's how come,"
and he don't traipse about no more, and the chillun teeter on th' edge of their feets, 'case they
wantsa laugh some more, but now the big folkses
solemn actin.

Me, well great day in the mornin, I get up and
trample on the bed with m'feet, hear, I cotch m'
breath so hard and feel so good. Whoo!

"You dassn't," Aunt Gastonia say to him, and
he say "Yes I do, and why do you say I dassn't?"
"Why?" Aunt Gastonia say, "and ain't you some
no-account man come in here and say you's gwine
take this sick chile away from the roof over his
head?"

"No roof of his own, Aunt Gastonia," he say, and that woman rare up and yell, "Don't Aunt Gastonia with *me* none, folks around know you's no-account and never did anything b'drink and traipse around the highway ever' blessed night and then jess up and leave when you most was needed by your po old folks. Go away, go away."

"Who that in the house?" Grandpa Jelkey yell, and fuss and pull at th'arms of his chair and look around. Well, you know, me and the chillun don't laugh no more now.

"Lady," say my brother, "how you talk," and Aunt Gastonia she yell, "Don't lady *me,* and don't come here fetchin no chile from outen my roof and learn him the ways of evil like you done learned from your pappy. YES," she yell, "you no better'n your pappy ever was and no better'n no *Jackson* ever was."

Well, I seed all about my life right then. "Who that man in the house?" yell Grandpa Jelkey, and he was so pow'ful mad I ain't never seed that old blind man so mad. He fetch up his cane and holt it tight. Well, right then here come Uncle Sim on the porch, and when that man see my brother standin in the middle of the house his eyes git big they's like chicken eggs, and white, and round, as hard. And he say soft, and p'culiar, "You ain't got no call bein in this house, man, and you knowed that." He don't turn away none but reach behind

the door and pull out that old shovel what's leaning there. "Git out of here." Aunt Gastonia cotch
her neck quick, and open her mouth to scream, but
ain't scarce ready yet, and ever'body wait.

5. SOME ARGUFYIN

WELL, YOU KNOW, my brother he ain't so scared of
Mr. Sim with his big old shovel, and say, "I ain't
pickin up this here chair to hit nobody with, nor
kill nobody 'cause I come here peaceable and
quiet, but I'm sure holdin on to this chair so long
as you hold that shovel Mr. Jelkey," and he holt up
that chair like the man with lion. His eyeballs get
red and he don't like so much none of this. Uncle
Sim, he look at him, then he look at Aunt Gastonia, and he say, "What's that boy doin here, tell
me, hear?"

And she tell him. And he say "Well then, hush
up woman," and he turn to my brother and say,
"Well go *on,* and go on mighty quick" and he point
out the door.

"Get him, Sim," Grandpa Jelkey yell, and he get

146

up from his chair again and holt out his cane, and yell, "Hit him over the head with the stick, boy."

"Sit that old man down," say Uncle Sim but Aunt Gastonia she start wailin and carryin on for me, 'case she don't wants me to leave with my brother, and she say, "No, Sim, no, that boy's sick and go hungry and cotch cold and ever' single thing in the world will happen to him and he'll turn bad, sinful bad, with that man, and the Lord shall drop it on my soul like the hot irons of hell and perdition, on your soul too, and on this house," and she say this rarin up most tearful and pitiful, for me to see, and come over to hold me and hide me from ever'body and kiss me all over. Whoo!

"Put on your clothes Pic," my brother say to me, and Uncle Sim put down the shovel, and my brother put down the chair, and Aunt Gastonia cry and cry, and holt me, poor woman, and I jess can't move an inch I'se so sorry t'see ever'thing come so mean and bad. Well, Uncle Sim, he come over and cotch Aunt Gastonia and pull her 'way from me, and my brother find my shirt and put it on me, and Aunt Gastonia shriek. Lordy, I find my shoes and I find my hole-hat and I'se ready to go, and brother fetch me up piggy-back, and here we go for the door.

Well then, what you supposed happened? Here come Mr. Otis' au-to licketysplit to the door, and out he come and knock on the house, and look in,

and say "Well what's this?" and look at ever'body
and push his hat back.

Well, here go ever'body talkin at the same time.
Aunt Gastonia, she argufy so hard, and explain so
loud, and pray so shriekly, ain't nobody else can
hear what's goin on, and Mr. Otis listen to her and
look at ever'body else most quiet, and don't say
nothin. Well, brother put me down 'case he can't
scarce stand there with me on his back whilst ever-
'body yell, and Mr. Otis take my wrist, and listen,
then he roll up m'eyeball like he done poor
grandpa and look in there, then he back up and
look me all over, and say, "Well, 'pears Pic's in
good enough health anyway. Now will you explain
ever'thing once around again for me?" and, after
Aunt Gastonia done that, and he shooked his head
yes, uh-huh, yes, uh-huh, he say, "Well, I don't
want to interfere with you folks but I don't guess I
was wrong when I said it wouldn't ever do to bring
the boy here, ma'm, and likewise don't guess he
can stay here." He look at Uncle Sim when he say
that, and Uncle Sim say, "Yes'r, I don't 'spect, Mr.
Otis, ain't been but trouble since he come here."
Then Mr. Otis go over and say hello to Grandpa
Jelkey, and Grandpa Jelkey say "I'se shore pleased
to hear your voice again, Mister Otis" and he jess
sit there grinnin from ear to ear 'case Mr. Otis
visitin.

Then Mr. Otis say, "I feel I owe it to this child's
grandaddy to see he's taken care of proper" and he

turn to my brother, and I don't reckon he like my
brother no more'n ever'body else, 'case he say, and
shake his head, "It don't 'pear to me like you can
take care of this child, neither. You got a *job* up
north?"

"Yes'r, I got a job," my brother say, and he
make a plain face and tuck his hat under his arm
again, but Mr. Otis don't 'pear to 'gree with him,
and say "Well, is that the only clothes you got to
wear when you travel?" and ever'body look at my
brother's clothes, which ain't much of a much, and
Mr. Otis say, "All you got there is a Army jacket,
and there's holes in the side of your pants, and
they don't fit right much anyhow because they're
all swole up at the legs and come down to your an-
kles so's I can't see how you can take 'em off, and
you've got a red shirt that ain't been washed, and
G.I. boots pretty well scraggly by now, and that
there *beret* on your head, so how do you ever expect me to believe you've got a job when you come
travelin on home like that?"

"Well sir," my brother say, "it's the *style* nowadays in NEW YORK," but that don't satisfy Mr.
Otis none, and he say, "Goatee and all? Well, I just
got back from New York City myself and I ain't
'shamed to say it was my first time up there, and I
don't think it's a fit place for folks to live whether
they be white or colored. I don't see any harm
takin care of your brother if you stay home, for
after all your grandaddy's house IS still standin

and you can get a job HOME as well as ever'where else."

"Well sir," my brother say, "I got a wife in New York," and Mr. Otis say quick "Does she work?" and my brother teeter a little bit on that, and say, "Yes, she works," and Mr. Otis say, "Well then who's goin to take care of this child durin the day?" and my brother get red in the eyeball again 'case he can't conjure up no more to say. Well, you know, I has my fingers crossed, 'case I be so pleased when my brother and me was headin for that door, and here I'se stopped dead in that old house again.

"He'll go to *school* in the daytime," my brother say, and give Mr. Otis a look all tuckered-out and s'prised from such some talk, and Mr. Otis, he smile, and he say "Well, I don't cast any doubt on your intentions, but who's goin to watch that child when he comes *home* from school in that NEW YORK *traffic?* Who's goin to help him cross the street in that coldhearted city, see he don't get run over by a truck and such-like? Yes, and where's that boy likely to get some *fresh air* to breathe? And proper friends that don't go about with knives and guns at fourteen? I ain't seen anything like it in all *my* born days. I don't aim to wish such a life on that boy, and don't guess his grand-daddy would neither in these last days of his, and I'm only doin this because I owe it at least to a very old friend of mine who taught me how to fish when I was no higher'n his knee. Well," and he turn to Aunt Gastonia, and heave a sigh all under him, "the only proper thing to do is put him in a good home till he's old enough t' decide for himself." And he pull out a fine book from his coat, and uncork a fine pen, and write most handsome inside it. "First thing in the mornin I'll call up and make whatever arrangements are necessary, and meanwhile the boy can stay here," and he turn to Aunt Gastonia, "because I'm sure, ma'm, you'll see that ever'thing is maintained proper." Yes, and Mr. Otis speak jess as fine and jess as pleasin as that.

But it ain't so pleasin to me none, 'case I don't like to stay in Aunt Gastonia's house 'nother minute, 'nother night, 'nother no time, nor go to no GOOD HOME like Mr. Otis said, nor see m'brother traipse off so lone and blue down the road like he done. Well, he look back over his shoulder, poor brother, ever' now and then, and dust up the sand slow with his ARMY BOOTS, and Aunt Gastonia's chillun they folly him a piece down the road 'case they like him so and wantsa see him shuffle and bow-down some more like he done in the house, but he don't. Mr. Otis stay on the porch talkin to Uncle Sim till my brother gone in the woods, then Mr. Otis get in his big au-to and go.

Well O well, they I was.

6. I GO THU THE WINDOW

COME NIGHTFALL EVER'BODY GO TO BED, and I'se in the bed with my th'ee little bitty cousins and can't sleep none, and say to myself, "Oh me, what happen to me next?" and I'se wearisome for ever-'thing and can't neither cry nor nothing no more. Ever'thing I fixed on done run out on me and wasn't nothin I could do. Lord, it was a bad long night.

Well, next thing I know I'se sleepin 'case I wake up and hear the hound dogs yelpin outdoor, and Uncle Sim open the window from where he sleep and sing out "Shet up that snappin and squallin out there," and Aunt Gastonia say, "What for the hound dogs cry?"

And Uncle Sim look, and come back in and say "Y'ere's a black cat spittin in the tree up yonder" and he go back to sleep. Aunt Gastonia she say, "Black cat go 'way from my do," and she make the sign, and go back to sleep likewise.

Then I hear m' little bitty cousin Willis what sleep by the window say "Who dat?" and I hear, ever so soft, "Shhh," and I look. Whooee, it's my brother in the window, and me and Willis creep up over little bitty Henry, and puts our noses to the screen, and then Jonas, he come too, and put *his* nose to the screen. "It the man done dance," say little Willis, and he go "Hee hee hee," but my brother put his finger on his mouth and say "Shhh!" Here ever'body listen close for Aunt Gastonia and Uncle Sim, and Grandpa Jelkey y'at sleep in the corner, but they jess sleepin and snorin, and the hound dogs whine so they don't hear nothin neither.

"What for you come here Mister Dancin Man?" say little Willis, and Jonas say "Uh-huh?" and little Henry wake up and say *"Git offen my laig!"* awful loud and ever'body jump back in the bed under the covers and m' brother duck down behind the window. Well, woof, you know, I hold up my breath then. But ain't nobody wake up.

Ever'body rare back up the window, soft.

"Is you gwine shuffle again?" Jonas say, and little bitty Henry he woke up and seed what was in the window, and rub his eye, and say, "Ish-yo-gin-shuff-gin?" 'case he always r'peats what Jonas say. My brother say "Shhh" and little bitty Henry put his finger to his mouth and turn around and nudge *me,* you know, like it was my foot, then ever'body look at my brother again.

"I'se come to get Pic," my brother say thu his hands, "but I come back tomorrow or next year and dance all over fo ever'one of you and give you each fifty cents, hear me now?"

"What fo you don't wantsa dance now?" little Willis say, and Jonas say "Jess a little bit?" and little bitty Henry say "Jiz-il-bit, hmm?" and my brother put his head on one side, and look at ever'body, and say, "Well, I do really b'lieve they's a Heaven somewhere," and he say, "Pic, git in your clothes quiet whilst I dance for these folks," and I do that quick and my brother he shuffle-up soft and dance in the yard in the moonlight and the chiles watch with a great big old s'prised grin on they faces. Well, you never seed such a dance like he done b'neath the moon like that, and no chiles like them seed one neither.

"Shet up that snappin and squallin out there!" yell Uncle Sim from t'other side of the house, and I tell *you,* ever'body duck down again s'fast nobody seed th' other do it. But Uncle Sim, he only mean the hounds, poor sleepin man.

Then ever'body raise up 'nother time again.

Brother undone the screen from the window and say "Shh" and reach in, and Jonas say "Shh" and little Henry say "S" and I cotch brother's neck, and out I go with my head first and then the feet, and dog my cats, and cat my dogs, and looky-here, if I ain't out in that barnyard in the middle of the dark and ready to leave and go.

"Less go," my brother say, and he haul me up on his back like he done in th' afternoon, and we turn around and look at the chiles in the window, and they's so sorry-lookin they's fixin to cry, you know, and my brother know this, and he say, "Don't cry, chillun, 'case me and Pic come back tomorrow or next year and we all have a big fine time t'gether and go down the crick and fish, and eat candy, and th'ow the baseball, and tell tales t' each other, and climb up the tree and *hant* the folks below, and *all* such fine things, you jess wait awhile, you jess see, y'hear me now?"

"Yas'r," Jonas say, and little Henry say, "Yass," and little Willis say "Uh-huh" and off me and m' brother go, 'cross the barnyard and over the fence and into the woods and don't make a sound. Whoo! We gone and done it.

7. WE COME TO TOWN

GRANDPA, IT WAS THE DARKENEST NIGHT 'case the moon got covered over by clouds jess as soon as brother and me reach the woods, and that moon was jess a scant banana moon and showed but scraggy and feeble betwixt the cloudy when it look out. It got cold, too, and I shore was chill. I reckon they was a rainstorm comin to warm me, 'case I don't at all feel so good as I done when we begun. Seem like they was somethin I forgot to do, or somethin I forgot to bring from back at Aunt Gastonia's house, but I knowed they was nothin like that, exceptin I all dreamed it. Lordy why'd I go dass dream such a thing and fret myself there? Way across the woods and thu the black yonder, here come the *train*, but it's pow'ful far off 'case me and brother only getsa hear it when the wind blow,

156

and hear it *wooo*—all long draw-out and goin away, sound like waitin for to get to the hills. Shoo! it was cold, and p'culiar, and black. But my brother, he don't mind.

He carry me thu the woods a space, then he put me down and say, "Woof, boy, I ain't goin to carry you on my back all the way to New York," and we tramp along till we get to the corn field, and then he say, "Here, you sure you can walk all right after bein sick like you was?" and I say "Yas'r, I'se jess a little chill" and walk along.

My brother say, "I get you a coat first thing," and then he say "Get up little boy," and he haul me up on his back again and look around at me out the corner of his eye. "Listen t' me, Pic" he say, "you're every bit sure you want to come along with me ain't you?" and I say "Yas'r."

"Well what for you call me *sir* when you know I'm your brother?"

"Yas'r" I say, and then I cotch myself and say "Yas'r, brother," and don't know what to say. Well, I reckon I was scared for I don't scarce know where we's goin and what happen to me when we get there if we gets there, and it don't sit right to myself to *ask* brother 'at come get me so glad and so pleased like that.

"Listen to me, Pic," he say, "you jess go along with me till we get home and call me *Slim* like ever'body else do, hear?"

"Yas'r, Slim" I say, and then I cotch myself again, and say "Yass, Slim."

"Well there you go" he laugh. "Now say, you seen that black cat back yonder in the Jelkeys' tree that had all them hound dogs barkin at it? I brung it there myself to make them dogs miss me, and didn't it spit, and fetch them up fine and bring us good luck that old black cat? Well, lookout!" Slim say to a tree, and dodge of it, and duck behind it, and bark at it, and go "Fsst!" like a cat, and both of us laugh some. That's the way *he* was, grandpa.

"Po little boy," he say, and give a sigh, and hitch me up higher on his back. "I guess you're as much scared of ever'thing like a grown man is. It's like the man say in the Bible—A fugitive and a vagabond shalt thou be in the earth. You ain't scarce eleven years old and already knowed that, I don't guess you didn't. Well, I come and made a vagabond out of you proper," and we walk along and come to see the lights of town up ahead, and he don't say nothin. Then here we go step on the road.

"Now, I'll tell you where we're goin," my brother say like if he read my mind and see all the troubles in it, and he say, "Then we'll unnerstand each other fine and be friends to go out to the world together. When I heard about grandpa I knowed all the trouble and shame that would come down on your head, Pic, and told Sheila, that's my wife, she'll be your new mother now, and she agreed with me and said—Go down get that poor chile. Well," he said, "Sheila's a mighty fine woman and you see pretty soon. So here I come down South for you 'case I'm the only kin you got left, and you're the only kin I got, baby. Now, you know why Mr. Otis give Grandpa Jackson that shack and that piece of land you was born on?— and why Mr. Otis wanted to help you today?"

"Nos'r, Slim" I say, and I shore wantsa hear it.

"Because your grandpa was born a slave and Mr. Otis' grandpa owned him once, you never knowed that did you?"

"Nos'r, Slim, nobody never told me that," I say, and seem to me I heard folks talk about *slave* one time, and it fetch up recollections, you know.

"Mr. Otis," my brother say, "he's a good man and feels he owes some of the colored folks some help now and then, and he has a nice way by him though it ain't by *me*, and mean well. Ever'body mean well, in their own pitiful way, and Aunt Gastonia mostly, poor woman. Uncle Sim Jelkey ain't no bad man, he's jess poor and can't support no vagabond Pics like you none. He don't too much hate anybody in his inside heart. Old Grandpa Jelkey, he's jess a old crazy man and I don't guess I'd—be crazy too if the same thing happened to me that happened to him. I tell you about that a minute. Well, I don't aim to see you go to no *foster home* like Mr. Otis was fixin to send you today.

Now, you know why Aunt Gastonia take you in but the menfolk Jelkeys don't want you?"

Well, I wantsa hear this, and I say "Why that?"

"That's because your daddy, Alpha Jackson, my daddy as well as yours, done blinded old Grandpa Jelkey in a fearsome fight about ten years ago and ain't nothin but bad blood left betwixt the two families. Aunt Gastonia, she was your mother's sister and loved your mother very much all her life, and took care of her right down the end when daddy come out of five years sentence in the work gang, three of 'em in the Dismal Swamp, and never did come back home to her."

"Where'd he go?" I ax my brother, and try to remember my father's face, but it wasn't no use.

"Nobody know," my brother say, and he walk along glum, and he say "Little man, your father was a *wild man* and a *bad man* and that's all he was, or is, and whether he's alive or dead and where-EVER he's at tonight. Your mother's long dead, poor soul, and nobody blamed *her* for becomin crazy and dyin like she done. Boy," my brother say to me, and turn his head to look at me, "you and me come from the *dark*." He said that, and said it jess as glum.

Well, here we come off the sand road and step on the most level and pleasin road I ever seed, and it's got white posts on the side with little bitty jewels shinin where the road go across the creek, and's got a fine white line painted in the middle of it and all such things. Well! And yonder straight ahead's all the lights of town, and here come three, four autos followin each other and havin a fine fast time, zoom, zoom, zoom.

"Well," my brother say, "you still want to come along with me?"

"Yas'r, Slim, I shore do wantsa go with you."

"Boy," he say, "you and me's hittin that old road for the WAY-yonder. Hey, lookout everybody, here we come," and ain't nobody 'round he say that to, but here we go jumpin down the road along two, th'ee white houses, both of us feelin so fine, and my brother say "Here we come to the outskirts of town" and wave his arm and yell "Wheee," and we hoop-de-doop along.

Here we go by a old white house as big as the woods in back of it, and the house got white poles and a porch mighty pleasin to see up front, and ever so many grand windows clear round back, and lights shinin from out the windows on the handsome grassy yard, and my brother say "Yonder's the ancestrial home of General Clay Tucker Jefferson Davis Calhoun retired hero of the Seventeenth Regimental Divisional Brigade of the Confederate Union 'at got hisself shot in the left side tibular tendon and got hisself stickpinned with a Gold Star Purple Honor of Congress medal and is now a hunnerd years old in his libr'y up yonder writin the Immemoriam Memories of the Gettysburg Shiloh Battle of Smoky Appamatoxburg, whoo!" and he carry on like that with ever'thing, and he don't care.

And here we go jumpin 'longside a regular house, and another regular house, then they's a whole heap of regular houses, and then they get un-regular and all red-rock color and lights pop up ever'where you see. Whoo! I never seed so many lights, and poles, and window-glass, nor so many people walkin on such even and fine roads. "This is town," my brother say, and well, you know, it seem to me jess 'bout then I seed this here TOWN a long time ago with my mother in a au-to, when we come to the movie show one time and I was lit-tle and small and couldn't guess to remember such things. And now here I was in town again, but I was growed-up and I was goin out to the *world* with my brother. Well, ever'thing began to be pow-'ful fetchin to watch at.

Here we turn thu a black old place and my brother say "This here's the alley you're goin to wait for me in whilst I get some sandwiches for the bus," and he put me down 'case he's all tucker out, and he take my hand and we walk. Here we come to the end of the alley, right across from a road at's all lit-up and brightly, but the alley it's in a shadow for me to wait in. "Yonder's the chicken shack," he say. "I'll go cross the street quick, and don't dass let nobody see you in case the Jelkeys done woke up and fix to send somebody find us, hear? Stand right here," he say, and push me agin the red-rock wall, and set me there, and then off he go toot across that *street*.

Well, grandpa, they I was with my back ain that wall, and look up at the sky betwixt it and th'other wall, and ever'where I turn my ear I hear au-tos, and folkses talkin, and all kind of noises and music, and I tell you, it was the noise of ever'body *doin somethin* at the same time all over with they hands and feet and voices, jess as plain. I never heard it before in the country, exceptin it come to my ear, jess like the water in the crick way yonder in the nighttime, swash, swash, and come most jumble-up and jolly. I'se so still and listenin, seem like *ever'body* doin somethin 'cept me. Across the street is that chicken shack, and it ain't nothin but a little bitty old shack jess like it say, but's got a most pow'ful bright light inside and they's men sittin in front of a long table-top, and they's eatin somethin 'at smell so *good* to me my mouth start waterin right where I is. They's a heap of radio music in there, and I can hear it clear across the street loud, hear the man sing: *"Where you been hiding baby, been looking everywhere, how come you treat me mean, can't you see I care?"* Well, it was fine radio music, the best I ever did hear, and come out of a big box with red and yaller lights turnin round in it. Over the door they was a wheel spin in a screen, and go humm, humm, and behind it a body could hear still another humm-humm from far away and it sound like a biggener wheel than that. Well, I reckon that was the *world wheel* I heard then. Wasn't it, grandpa? Oh, I was jess pleased.

I say to myself, "I jess take two step-ups this *alley*," and I move up along the wall and come to see more of the street. Whoo! It shore was brightly and pleasin.

Then here come my brother out of the chicken shack with a paper bag in his hand, and here come a bunch of men along the street, and they see him and yell, "Hey there Slim, what you doin down from NEW YORK?" And he yell, "Hello there Harry, and hello there Mr. Redtop Tenorman, and hello there Smoky Joe. Well, what you boys up to?" and they say, "Oh, we jess draggin along, you know." And he say, "Ain't heard you boys jump in a *long* time," and they say "Oh, we jump now and then. Say, how you make it with that mustache on your chin?" My brother say, "Oh, jess goin along tryin to have a good time, you know," and they say "Well hey now" and go off down the street and ever'body say see you later.

Yes, I shore liked town and never knowed it was so lively.

Me and brother sneak on down the alley and back to the skirts of town, and skedaddle along feelin good 'case we gets to eat some of them sand-wiches soon and 'case brother say we wait for the *bus* by the *junction,* and that bus it's about due any minute, and when we get on that bus I won't be cold no more, and he won't neither. "Bus station ain't no place for us tonight, boy," he says to me, and he say "Oh well, oh well, and who cares, I guess it's all the same when you believe in the Lord like I do, now say, You hear me Lord?"

And we sit on the white posts with the shiny buttons in em and wait 'bout half an hour for the bus, or two half hours, I don't recollect.

Here it come. It come big and brawly in the road, and said "WASHINGTON" on it, and the man at the wheel jam down the speed to stop for us, and it go zoom-boom right by us like it NEVER stop, and spit sand and wind and a old hot smell in my face, but stop yonder jess for us, and we run for it. Well, when I seed that big machine I said to myself "Ain't nobody know where *I'm* goin in this thing but my brother watch over me from now on."

I never see Aunt Gastonia no more now.

8. THE BUS GO UP NORTH

GRANDPA, ain't gonta tell too much about the bus 'case a heap of doins was croppin up in NEW YORK, and I didn't have no notion about em in that bus, and jess gawked, you know.

Well, brother and me paid the man some money, then we walked back thu the people in the seats and ever'body look at us and we look at them, then we sit down in the back sofa, only it ain't rightly a soft sofa, and there we sit lookin straight ahead over ever'body's head at the driver, and he turn off the light and zoom-up the bus, and faster and faster we go with two big old lights leadin us the way thu the land. Brother fall asleep right away, but I stayed awake. I reckon we left *North Carolina* after 'bout a half hour, or two half hours, 'case the road done change from black to

166

brown and on each side of it I didn't get to see no more houses but jess the wilderness. I guess it was jess great big old woods without no houses, and dark? and black? and jess as solemn? It was the *wilderness* Aunt Gastonia pray about when she pray agin it so loud.

And here come the rain pourin down on that wilderness, and the road run wet and lonesome right thu it.

It was a scarifyin thing to see and make a body glad he's in a bus with a whole lot of people.

I watched ever'body all night long, but they was most sleepin in their chairs and it was too black to see, and I tried to see, but it wasn't no use. I shore didn't wantsa go to sleep that night.

I say to myself "Pic, you're going to *New York* now, and ain't it somethin, now ain't it?" and I prod myself, and feel good.

And I got all sleepy p'culiar in m'eyes 'case I sleep this time of the evenin back home here, and over to Aunt Gastonia's too, so next thing I know I jess has to sleep, and that's all I done that night.

Come 'bout mornin I look up and see where I am, in the *bus,* and can't believe it, and say to myself "Now that's why I'se bouncin so dadblame much." And I look over to brother, and he's still sleepin and's got the whole back sofa to hisself and's all stretched out loose and peaceful, and I'se pleased to see him sleep so 'case I know he must be tired. And I look out the window.

And you know, I never seed anything so pow'ful grand and big, and I seed pow'fuller and grander things since then, all the way to *Californy*. What I seed then was jess like when the first time I seed the *world* I tell you. It was a great river with a tree shore on both sides, and poureds a whole power of water betwixt the land about a mile long, and then it spread out yonder all flat I guess for to pass off to the *sea*. Way yonder on a hill they was a big old white house with posts on the porch like I seed the night before, a *ancestrial* home of a General retired hero of Appamatoxburg like brother said, and on the other side of the river I seed a grand and fearsome housetop, all white and round and jess like a handsome cup upside down, with little bitty far away trees and tiny little roofs rounderneath it. The man in front said to his wife, "Yonder's the Capitol dome darling" and point to it, and that's what it was. And they was the finest, softenest wind blew in from the land to the river, and make ever'thing ripple and jump in the water all over, most peaceful. The sun shine on that grand fine Capitol dome and hit flush on a streamer 'at's tied to a gold pole way on top of it, and do it dazzly, too. All that land I told you we done roll over in the bus all night, here we was in the middle of it, 'case they *never* was a town so white and so laid out grand, and brother woke up and said "This here is the city of *Washington* the nation's capitol where the President of the United States of Amer-

ica and ever'body is," and he rub his eyes, and I
look close and can see they's a heap of things goin
on yonder in Washington 'case I hear it hum all
over when the bus slow down at the river red light
and I put my head out the window to watch. Well,
and I never seed such a big sky, and so many fine,
solemn clouds as passed over Washington of the
United States 'at mornin.

After that, grandpa, I didn't get to sleep much. It
was mighty hot inside the city of Washington when
we stopped there and had to change to another bus
'at said NEW YORK on it, and crowded? Ever-
'body in the world lined up for that New York bus,
and sat inside sweatin. I couldn't sleep no more except on brother's arm, and had to sit up straight in
that back sofa and drop my head over most un-
comfortable, and his poor shoulder was so hot.
Busdriver man say "Baltimore next stop," but run
off to do somethin else instead and don't come
back f'the longest time. Well, I wished we was
back on that NIGHT bus in the WILDERNESS.
Babies was cryin all up and down the bus, and felt
jess as bad as I did I guess. I look out the window
and all I see is the wall on one side, and the wall
th'other side, and the sun beat down on the roof,
and whew! it was so daggone hot I was sickish. I
say to myself "Why don't nobody open a window
in here?" and I look around and ever'body's
sweatin but don't make a move for the window. I
say to Slim "Less open a window or we's dead."

And Slim pull and tug and rassle at that window, but can't bulge it one bit. "Phew!" he say. "This must be one of them *modern air-conditioned* buses. Phew!" Slim say "Less go, bus, and blow some air in here." And a man up front turn around and give us a look, then *he* try to open *his* window, and can't bulge it, and sweat and cuss over it. Here come a big soldier-man and he reach out and give that window one big pull-up, and it don't bulge none. So ever'body look straight ahead and go on sweatin.

Well, you know that busdriver man come back and seed Slim pullin some more at that window, and he said "Please leave the windows alone, this happens to be an air-conditioned bus" and he turn on a button up front when he start the bus, and I tell you the finest cool air began to blow all over that bus, only thing is, ever'body got *cold* in a minute and the sweat turns on me like ice water. So Slim, he tugged at that window again to get some *hot air* back in, but couldn't do it, and we look thu the window at them beautiful green fields, and Slim said they was MARYLAND, and wished he was settin in the sunny grass. I reckon ever'body felt the same way too.

Grandpa, travelin ain't the easiest and pleasingest thing in the world but you shore gets to see many innerestin things and don't go 'bout it backwards neither.

When we got to *Philadelphia* folks got out the

bus and me and Slim got ourselves a new seat
smackdab up front in the driver's window, and
bought-up some ice-cold soda orange and ain't
nothin better when you feel sickish. Slim said "We
can sit up front now because we crossed the
Mason Dixie line," and I axed him what that was,
and he said it was the line of the law for *Jim Crow,*
and when I axed him who Jim Crow was, he said
"That's you, boy."

"I ain't no Jim Crow anyhow," I told him,
" 'case you know my name is Pictorial Jackson."

"Oh," says Slim, "is that so? Well, I never
knowed that, uh-huh. Looky-here Jim," he said,
"don't you know about the law that says you can't
sit in the front of the bus when the bus runs below
the Mason Dixie line?"

"What for you call me Jim?"

"Now Jim!" he says, and cluck-cluck at me solemn. "You mean to tell me you don't know about
that line?"

"What line?" I say. "I ain't seed no such a line."

"What?" he say. "Why, we just crossed it back
there in Maryland. Didn't you see Mason and
Dixie holdin that line across the road?"

"Well," I says, "did we run over it or underneath
it?" and I'se tryin to recollect such a thing but jess
cain't. "Well," I say, "I guess I musta been sleepin
then."

And Slim laugh, and push my hair, and slap his
knee. "Jim, you kill me!"

"What did that line look like?" I axed him, 'case I wasn't old enough to know it was a joke yet, you see. Well, Slim said he didn't know what such a line looked like neither on account he never seed it any more than I did.

"But there *is* such a line, only thing is, it ain't on the *ground,* and it ain't in the air neither, it's jess in the head of Mason and Dixie, jess like all other lines, border lines, state lines, parallel thirty-eight lines and iron Europe curtain lines is all jess 'maginary lines in people's heads and don't have nothin to do with the ground."

Grandpa, Slim said that jess as quiet, and didn't call me Jim no more, and said to hisself "Yes sir, that's all it is."

The busdriver man come back, and said "All aboard for NEW YORK" and like I tell you 'bout *travelin* and not goin backwards, we jess went *forwards.* Whoo! Straight ahead was that New York road, and all the traffic of the cars cuttin in and out, zoom, zip, but that driver man jess sit at that wheel 'thout movin a muscle and look right ahead and push his big machine straight on thu as fast as he can go. Anybody come out of a side street and see us comin, why they jess freeze right up and let us come by. That bus man jess cleared the way for hisself, *he* don't care. The others don't care neither 'case they jess barely miss us and go zip thisaway and zip thataway after they miss. I reckon his bus couldn't *ever* stop if somebody got dead in the way.

and then you couldn't find their pieces if he did, and couldn't look for the pieces except in the next county. Grandpa, you never seed such drivin and breezin along and ever'body so nonchalant about it, and so sure. I tell you, I couldn't look.

Slim, he was asleep again and this time his head dropped on my arm jess like mine done on his arm in Washington, and slept like that with his eyes closed right in front of the window and here's that bus man carryin him on thu all that road jess as faithful as you please. Slim wasn't scairt none, nor flinched awake or asleep. Well, I shore did love him a whole lot jess then, and said to myself, "Pic, you had no call bein scairt last night when he come and carried you thu the woods and told you not to worry. Now, Pic, you gotsa grow up this minute for Slim. You ain't no country boy *now*."

So I look straight ahead thu the window, and there we go north to NEW YORK in that tremenjous bus.

9. FIRST NIGHT IN NEW YORK

NOW I GOTSA TELL YOU 'BOUT EVER'THING happened in New York and how it happened so fast I jess barely had time to see what New York was like. You see, we come in I believe May 29th to stay and three days later we was all balled up and got to go on the road again, so you see how quick people has to live up in New York and how we was.

When I seed New York was from that bus, and Slim poked me up from the seat and said "Here we are in New York" and I looked and the sun was *red* all over, I looked again, and rubbed my eyes to wake up, for grandpa, we was goin over a long big bridge at run over a whole sight of rooftops and all I has to do is look down to see the chillun runnin betwixt the houses below, Slim said it wasn't New

174

York yet, jess the HOBOKEN SKYWAY he said, and pointed up ahead to show me New York. Well I jess could barely see a whole heap of walls and lanky steeples way, way off yonder all cloudy inside the smoke. Then I looked all round, and grandpa, it was the most monstrous and tremenjous stretch of rooftops and streets, and bridges and railroads, and boats and water, and great big things Slim said was *gas tanks,* and walls, and junkyards, and power lines, and in the middle of it set this old swamp 'at's got tall green grass and yaller oil in the water, and rusty rafts long the shore. It was a sight like I never dreamed to see. And here come more of it where we turn the bridge, and ever'thing's so smoky and tremenjous, and so laidout far I can't watch at some least littlest point of it without I see some more heaped up yonder behind it in the fog and smoke. Well grandpa, and that ain't all:—I told you the sun was red, and that was 'case jess then the sun was peekin thu a big hole in the clouds up in Heaven, and was sendin down great long sun-fingers ever'whichway from the hole, and it was all jess so rosy and purty like if'n God come down thu the smoke to see the world. Well jess before I woked up I guess ever'body in New York done put on they lights, and I guess it was dark then, on account now all them lights they put on was caught feeble and strange in the red sunlight and ever'where I look was them po lights burnin up 'lectricity for nothin, deep inside the

streets and the alleys, up on the walls, up on top
the bridges, thisaway in the awful fog and thataway on the soft rosy water, and they jess tremble
and shake jess like ever'thing's a big old campfire
folks done lit before sundown and didn't dass put
it out yet, 'case they knowed it wasn't no real day
for long. Well, next thing you know, the sun turn
purple and blue and leave jess one peel of fire on
the cloudbank, and it gets almost dark.

Slim say, "Ah me it's May again. Wish't I could
go someplace tonight," and I say "Ain't we goin no
place?"

And he say, "I mean *someplace* where all the
boys and girls have their fun. Ain't never seen nor
found such a place all my born days. It's what
them boys is thinkin 'bout right now."

"What boys is that?" I say, and he point to New
York and say "The boys in the jailhouse tonight."
Grandpa, I axed him last time if he was in the jailhouse in New York and he said yes, he was *busted*
one time but he didn't do nothin wrong, his friend
did. He said his friend was in that jailhouse still,
and wasn't no better than him.

Well, now I told you how fearsome and grand
New York was when I first seed it, and that ain't
all. The bus come down into a tunnel and whoosh!
it and ever'body else go barrelin along the walls,
and it warn't dark in there but *bright* as you like
and all lit-up jolly. "Now we's under the Hudson
River," brother say, "and wouldn't it be somethin

if that river bust thu and come down on our heads?" I didn't dass guess 'bout that till we come out the other side, and when we did I plum forgot to guess, and I reckon most folks is like that, ain't they grandpa, till the day such a thing happen to them? The bus come out that LINCOLN TUNNEL it was called, and a great yaller light shine up the front of it, and ain't nobody but one man walkin on the street, and I look at him and he look at me too. Well, I guess that man said to hisself "There's a little boy comin to New York for the first time and cain't do nothin but gawk at a man like me 'at's so busy in New York and got so many things to do."

And here we was in New York, and it didn't look half grand now we was inside it on account you couldn't see far with all them *walls* risin clear up on every side. Well you know, I look straight up oncet and I look again and don't see but the most p'culiar brown air in the sky above the tall walls, and I seed it was on account all the lights of New York paint-up the nighttime way high yonder, and do it so much it don't need no more'n a few feeble stars in it. "Them's skyscrapers," Slim said when he seed me look up. Well then the bus turn on a big street, Slim said it was Thirty Four street then I seed plenty far and a whole great gang of folks and grandpa it was jess so many lights strung out one after 'nother, and up, and down, and trembly along the walls, and red, and blue, and all the folks and the car traffic acting jess like ants as far as your eye can see. Grandpa, all the folks you do see, and things they do, and all the streets you do see, and the places there is, and whilst you gotsa keep in mind all the folks and streets you don't see, at's round the corner and way yonder ever'whichaway, and *up* in the skyscrapers, and *down* in the subway —well, you can see how t'ain't pos'ble to make a body unnerstand it lessen they done come and looked for theirselves.

The bus stop, and me and Slim got off and went down the street to the *subway,* which is a tunnel train there underneath New York at ever'body takes to git where they's goin the fastenest best way. "Bus is fast in the country but's too slowed-up in *this* town," Slim say. We pay the man when we pay the gate-machine, and get on the train when the door-machine bring the door open, and get inside and set and let the train-machine run along the rail. Wasn't nobody around to run the doggone thing 'case I looked up front and wasn't nobody steerin it. And I *knowed* we went fast and I wasn't fooled by no dark.

Brother and me got off at Hundred Twenty Five street in *Harlem.*

"We's just around the corner from home, old-timer," Slim say to me, "so you see we made it after all." Well then we come upstairs on the street and it's all as jolly and brightly as Thirty Four street, and grandpa, here we was a *hunnerd* streets

up along the city, so you can see how New York
never gets to be near the country as you go along
it.

"Stand right still whilst I wash your face for
Sheila," Slim said, and he stopt me on the street in
front of the water-bubbler and rub off my mouth
with his handkerchief and great big crowds of folks
walks by and it's a nice warm night again and I
shore feels glad we come to New York. "Slim," I
say, "I's shore glad I ain't at Aunt Gastonia's no
more and won't be scairt neither no more." And I
look down the street where we come from and say
to myself, "No, North Carolina ain't round here
no more."

"Well thass the way to talk, soldier," Slim say,
"and just because ever'thing's so fine I'm gonta
buy Sheila a little thing in the store here so's we'll
all have a fine time our first night home."

And we go into a *record store* at's full of men
fishin through the record racks and jumpin up and
down while they do so like they jess can't wait.
Ain't nothin but music and noise in there, and a
whole bunch of men out front jumpin jess the same
way. Whoo, what fun! Slim, he went fishin and
jumpin like ever'body else, and come up with a
record, and yelled "Whee! Look what I found!"
and ran to the man and throwed him a dollar.
Then we go around the corner to a street at wasn't
so bright but jess as gay and full of folks in the

dark, and run upstairs into a old crumbly hallway, and knock on the door and push it in.

Well, there was Sheila, and I liked her jess as quick as I laid my eyes on her. She was a slim purty gal 'at wore glasses with red horn rims, and a purty red sweater, and purty green skirt, and fine jigglets on her wrists, and when we come in she was standin at the stove makin coffee and readin the paper all at the same time, and looked at us s'prised.

"Baby!" Slim yelled out, and run up and hugged her, and spun her round, and kissed her smack upon the mouth, and said "Looky yonder your new son, mother dear, ain't he somethin fine?"

"Is that Pic?" she said, and come over and took both my hands, and lookt at me down in the eve. "I can see you've been havin lots of trouble lately haven't you, little boy," she said, and I don't know how she could tell that, but she did, and I tried to smile to show I liked for her to be so nice but I was jess a little too bashful. "Well won't you smile sometime?" she said, and I had to go freeze there so foolish and said but jess "Uh-huh" and look away. Doggone it!

Then she said "Wasn't that chile cold comin up here in that little sweater full of holes? And look at his socks, they're full of holes too. Even his poor pants in the back here."

"My hat too," I said, and showed her my hole-hat.

Well, I caught her then and it was her 'at didn't
know whether to laugh or look awful, and she got
red and laughed. I reckon, grandpa, it was because
a boy like me ain't got no call talkin about himself
when a lady's doin that for him, ain't it? Well, she
was the finest soul, and I knowed it jess then by the
way she got red and didn't mind.

Slim said "I'll buy him clothes first thing in the
mornin," and Sheila said "How you gonna do that
without money?" but he jess started that new record on the record machine in the corner and you
shoulda seen him clap his hands and walk up and
down with his feet right where he was, and shake
his head and say "Oh where's my horn tonight? Oh
where's my horn tonight?" over and over, and look
up and laugh, 'case he likes the music so much,
and say "Play that thing *Slop*jaw!" Grandpa, that
record was by Slopjaw Jones done with a saxo-
phone horn and everybody yellin and bangin the
piano behind him, and you never heard such reck-
less jumpin and crashin in your ears out there in
the country. Seem like the folks up in the city
wants to have fun and ain't got time for no worry
exceptin when worry catches up with them, that's
when they ain't busy about worryin.

"What do you mean no money?" Slim said, and
Sheila said, "I don't like to tell you and Slopjaw,
and everybody, and Pic here, but I went and lost
my job day before yesterday because they're tearin
down the building where the restaurant was down

on Madison avenue and puttin up a new office building."

"Office building?" Slim yelled. "Did you say *office* building? What's they goin to do with a *office* building? Ain't nobody get to *eat* in no office building."

"You talk silly," Sheila said, and look at him sad. "Why shoo, all they've got to do is go round the corner to eat in a restaurant."

"Then they put up another office building *there* and then where do you go?" said Slim, and then heaved a sigh. "Doggone it, what are we goin to do now?" He turned off the record, and looked round the kitchen, and began walkin up and down in it, and worried himself to death. I seed then how Slim had worried before about a lots of things. His face dragged down awesome and his eyes jess went starin straight ahead and his bones of his face stuck out from his cheeks and made him look old. Poor Slim, I never forget *that* look on his face when I think about him now. "Dog-*gone*," he jess say, over and over, "dog-*gone*." Then he look at Sheila and she didn't know it but his face flinch a little bit like if they was pain way down deep in his heart, and he come back to say "Dog-*gone!*" and be starin straight ahead after that, and for a long awesome time. Lord, Lord, Slim always tried so hard to explain to me and ever'body else the things on his mind, like he done then. "Dog-gone it, are we goin to be beat all the time or *ever* make a livin

around here? When will our troubles end? I'm
tired of bein poor. My wife is tired of bein poor. I
guess the *world* is tired of bein poor, because *I'm*
tired of bein poor. Lord a mercy who's got some
money? I know *I* ain't got some money and that's
for sure, now look" and show his empty pocket.

"You shouldn't of bought that record," Sheila
said.

"Well," he said, "I didn't know then. Now so
where'd this money go that folks is supposed to
live on? I'd jess be satisfied if I had a field of my
own I could jess grow things in and wouldn't need
no money, and wouldn't worry *what* folks had it.
not records neither. But I ain't got a field and I
need money to eat. Well where am I goin to get
this money? I gotsa get a job. Yes, a job, gotsa get,
I-got-a-git-a-job. Sheila," he call out, "first thing in
the mornin I am goin out and find me a job. You
know how I'm sure I can get one? Because I need
one. You know why I need a job? Because I ain't
got no money." And he went on like that, and got
hisself all 'volved in talk, and come round again to
worry some more. "Sheila, I shore hope I get a job
tomorrow."

"Well," Sheila said, "I'll have to look for one
too."

"It's so hard to get a job that you can't stick to
all your life," Slim said. "I wish I could get a job
playin tenor in a club and make my livin that way,
and express myself with that horn. Show ever'body

how I feel by the way I play, and make them see
how happy I can be and ever'body can be. Make
them learn how to enjoy life and do good in life
and unnerstand the world. A whole lot of things.
Play sometimes about God, by the way I can make
my horn pray in the blues and get down on my
knees to signify. Play in such a way as to show
ever'body how hard a man tries all the time, and
make somebody learn *that*. I want to be like a
schoolteacher with that horn, or like a preacher,
but show ever'body that jess a musician can do so
simple a thing as take a horn in his hand, and blow
in it, and finger the stops, yet be a preacher and a
schoolteacher in the *result* of what he's doin. I tear
my heart out wherever I go. All over this country
I've been, and ain't been liked because I was colored, by people who don't mind their own personal
business, and don't want me to do good, but I've
tore my heart out with that horn. That horn is the
only way people come to listen to me. They won't
talk on the street, but they'll clap and yell hooray
when I'm on the bandstand, and smile at me. Well
I smile back, I ain't cool about people, nor cool
about nothin. I like to respond and listen and be
with people. I feel good most of the time, and do it.
Lord a mercy, I sure wantsa live and have my
place in the world like they call it and I'm ready to
work if I can only work with my horn, because
that's the way I like to work and I don't know how
to run a machine. Well, I ain't learned yet anyway,

and like my horn better, I do. Ar-tist, I'm a ar-tist,
jess like Mehoodi Lewin and the columnist in the
paper and whoozit. I got a million ideas and can
shore pour them out of that horn, and I ain't doin
so bad pourin them without the horn. Sheila," he
say to her, "less eat some supper and worry about
ever'thing tomorrow. I'm hungry and want my
strength back. Throw some beans in there, and
after supper make a lunch for tomorrow noon-
time."

"I'll have to make one for myself," Sheila said,
and then they wondered what was to happen to me
tomorrow, and Slim decided for me to go with him
to look for work and we could eat the lunch together. "Make it a big one. You got *bread?* Throw
somethin between that bread and that'll be fine.
Wished we had a coffee mug. You got a coffee
mug? Thermidor you say? Well, *thermidor* it shall
be, with the coffee hot. Pic," he said to me, "you
and me ain't even started travelin together is we?
We just come four and fifty miles and here we go
again. Eat, then we go to sleep and get up early.
Got a nice old sweater of mine for you tomorrow,
and clean socks. Well, we'll make it again. Here we
go. Ladies and gentlemen, look out. *Look out for
your boy!*" he shouted, and closed his eyes a minute, and stood like that.

Well, that was the first night in New York, and
shore 'joyed the supper, and us sittin round the
table till ten at night, talkin and recollectin and

Sheila told about when she was my age in *Brooklyn*, and all such fine things went on of gabbin together in the nighttime, and me lookin forward to what happen next ever'time I look out the window at New York. I say to myself, "Pic, you left home and come into *New York!*"

I had me a fine cot-bed to sleep on all night.

But that next day wasn't so pleasin as this first night.

10. HOW SLIM LOST
TWO JOBS IN ONE DAY

I'LL NEVER FORGET THAT DAY because so many things happened all at oncet. Started off, me and Slim got up jess as the sun come back red, and he cooked up some eggs and breakfast so's Sheila could sleep some more. Grandpa, ain't nothin better in the world like eggs and breakfast in the mornin because your taster ain't worked all night and ever'thing comes so chawy and smells so fryin good it makes a body wish he could eat ever-'body's breakfast all up and down the street seven times, ain't it the truth? When we come down on the street and I seed all them men eatin more eggs and breakfast in the corner store I wished I could eat all the breakfasts in *New York City*. It was a cool mornin and wasn't but six o'clock. I had my new socks, and Slim's black sweater, and Sheila done sewed up the holes in my pants, and I was all set. And you know the first thing happened? We was standin in the doorway and Slim was readin the newspaper *want ads,* and it was mighty chill, and keen, and ever'body come by to get to the work-bus coughin and spittin and shore looked mis'ble from work in New York City, and some of them was readin the papers with the most gloomy disappointed look like if'n the papers complained jess what they hankered to see, and here come a man out of that crowd who knew Slim. "Well there *daddyo,*" he said, and showed Slim the palm of his hand, and Slim showed him his, and they touched up like that. "Don't tell me you're lookin for a job again," the man said, and Slim told him he was shore enough.

"Well, I declare, I got a job for you. You know my brother *Henry.* He ain't got up yet this mornin. I jess talked to him. I say *Henry,* ain't you supposed to go to work in that cookie factory down on whatzit street? And he hid under the pillow and says, yes I guess so, uh-huh, but don't move a bone. I say *Henry,* ain't you gettin up? *Henry!* Well now *Henry?* Hey, yoo-hoo, *Henry?* That man just made up his mind to sleep, that's all," and Slim's friend walked off ten feet and come back again.

"Do you think he'll be fired?" Slim axed him curious, and the man said "*Henry?* Will *he* be fired?" Dog my cats if he don't walk off again and come back. "You mean *Henry?*" and he looked away, and shook his head, and felt too tired to do anything but hang his head. "Shooee, he's got the *world record* for that. He's been fired more times than he's been hired."

"What's the address of this place?" Slim said, and the man knew it and gave it to us, and made another couple funny jokes and said "Lookout for the boogieman" when me and Slim took off for the job factory. Well, he was all right.

We took the subway, then walked down a street to the river and there was the cookie factory. It was jess a great big old place with chimbleys and lots of machines thunderin inside, and gave out a mighty sweet smell that made us smile. "Why this will be a good job," Slim said, " 'cause it smells so good," and we jumped up the steps and come in the office. The boss was there by the punchin clock and was wonderin where was *Henry,* I guess. We waited on a bench a half hour, then the boss said Slim had better start workin all right because nobody was never goin to show up. Slim had to spend some time writin papers, so he told me to wait in the park across the street till noon and then come in for lunch with him. And there he was straight into a job right off quick.

"Sheila'll be happy," I said to myself, and knowed it.

I waited all mornin in that park. It was a tiny park with a iron rail and some bushes, and swings, and such, and jess sat most of the time watchin at a couple other children, and figurin life. I made friends with a little white boy who came into the park with his mother. He was all fine lookin in a blue suit with gold buttons, and knee high stockins, and a red huntin hat. He had a most admirable way of talkin and settin hisself on the bench. His mother read a book on the other bench and smiled at us kindly.

"And why are you waitin here?" he axed me, and I said "My brother works in that factory over yonder."

He says "Why do you say *over yonder,* are you from Texas in the West?"

"Texas in the West?" I said. "No, I don't come from up there, I'm from North Carolina." "Are there any cowboys there?" he axed, and I lied and said there was, and we talk. I liked that boy a whole lot. We'd a talked more but he had to go home quick. We was fixin to have a race but he left. Why, he had the goldenest hair and the clearest blue eyes, and I never seed him again.

Well at noon I went up to the factory, and seed Slim by the window with a shovel. All I had to do was sit on a barrel outside the window which was open, and watch Slim till it was time for us to eat.

Well, he was workin so fast he didn't even see me, and when he did, all he had time to do was yell. He bent over with the shovel, and dug into a truckload of fudge, and heaved it up on a belt that rolled around from wheels and carried the fudge clear down the other end of the factory. Before it hit a big roller Slim flatted out the fudge with his hands, then it rolled under and got to be like a sheet of fudge, and then got pieced full of holes by a knife machine 'at jabbed down and made cookies. Slim had to shovel up and then drop the shovel and hurry to use his hands, so's he never could stop one minute because the belt kept turnin. One time he blew his nose and the man down the way said "Send up some more of that chocolate," thass how fast ever'body worked and the rollers rolled. The sweat jess fell from Slim's head and fell in the fudge, and he couldn't do nothin about it, had no time to dry himself. Then a man rolled up another truckload of fudge, only this time it was *vanilla* and all white and purty, and Slim jess stuck that old chocolate shovel in there and hauled it up, all streaky. When he spread the fudge with his hands he looked straight ahead and said "Phew!" because that was the only time he stoop up straight enough to talk to himself. That shore was some hard job and I knowed it.

Slim yelled to me "If I stop one second my arms are going to knot up round my neck from Charley Horse!" and jumped back in the fudge. One time he said "Ow!" and one time he said "Whee!" and another time I heard him say "Oh Lord a mercy, I'll never eat a cookie again."

Twelve o'clock, a big whistle blew and all the

machines slowed down and ever'body walked off. But Slim, he only leaned there on the post and wiped his head and looked at his hands. Next thing you know, his right hand curled up and reached around for his wrist, and he said it was a *cramp*. Then half of his whole arm curled up like he was showin his muscles, but he wasn't, it was jess another cramp, and he pushed it back and forth and looked at it, and sighed, and cussed.

Well, he came out and we ate the lunch on the office steps in the hot sun. "I hope my arms are better for this afternoon," he said, and was glum and didn't say much more, even when I told him about the little boy I met. Come about one o'clock that big whistle blew again and Slim went back to work.

I watched again. Well, you know, that poor man couldn't grip the shovel when he reached for it, his fingers was so stiff. When he did close his fingers over it his arms began to shake and had no strength in them, and he couldn't hold the shovel at all. The man down the fudge-belt yelled "Start up that vanilla will you? We ain't got all day." Slim called out to the boss and showed him his arms. Both of them stood shakin their heads and thinkin about this, because it *was* sad, and Slim tried again to grip the shovel and couldn't do it, and the boss rubbed his arm some, but Slim jess couldn't control his arms no more. They were red, and hot, and hurt him. Well, he wiped his hands with a rag, and

they talked some, then by and by Slim came out
the office door and joined me.

"What happened?" I axed him.

"I jess can't work any more today, my arms is
tied in a knot." And that's all he said, and we went
home with one mornin's pay in a envelope, $3.50.

Sheila came home at five o'clock, and hadn't
found a job. Slim told her what happened and we
ate supper most silent.

Well, it was the first time I seen Slim gloomy.

"Well I'll tell you," he said after supper, and jess
soaked his hands in the hot water, "I don't like
them kind of jobs like I had today. I can't shovel
fast enough to keep with no rollin belt like that and
I used to be a prizefighter too. I don't like to sink
my hands in no whole tub of fudge. Do you make
your own cookies, gal, or buy it? Shoo, what's I
goin to do with a thirty-five-dollar paycheck *any-*
how when the groceries theirselves cost about
twenty, and the rent's took up the rest. I can't be
shovelin that doggone stuff up and down myself
just so's ever'body can't pay extra bills and can't
buy a hat, and my arms get so tired they hang like
a broken branch in the tree. I don't want to complain all the time, but shucks almighty no matter
how much I love the world and get my kicks every
live-long day, and I think Pic here loves the world
and gets his innocent joys every day, and you love
the world and feel fine in the mornin, it jess ain't
the same when there's no dough and the house is

black with money debts. It's like a closet you have to sit in, doggone it, 'stead of a house."

"Well, you're just tired today," said Sheila, and she kissed him on the ear and gave him a fine purty sidelook, and trotted off to make coffee on the stove. I reckon Sheila loved Slim like she was his slave. He didn't have to do anything but sit there, and Sheila loved him fine, and watched him, and never passed him in the house without she touched him and sometimes winked at him.

Well, it was mostwise a glum evenin, like you can see, but somethin else happened jess then.

A tall man all well dressed and smilin come in the door, and whoopeed:—"Slim you old tadpole," and ever'body began laughin and forgot their troubles for then. "You know why I'm here, man?" said the man, his name was Charley, and Slim lit up bright and said "You mean?"

"Yes, thass right, a job, and not only that I got a *horn* for you."

"A horn? A horn? My kingdom for a horn! Less go!" and we all went downstairs to the street. Some other man was in the car that had the horn in it, and Slim took the horn out the case and blooped in it a little bit, right on the sidewalk, and felt jess grand. "Where we blow?" he said, and Charley said it was at the Pink Cat Club. "Do I have to wear a suit?" Charley said he shore did have to because the boss man at the Pink Cat was jess complete persnickity about such things and wouldn't pay Slim no five dollars if he didn't like him.

"Well *hoe-down!* Here we go for five dollars Sheila baby," Slim said, and ran upstairs as fast as he could run to put on his suit. Sheila hurried and put on a nice dress, and brushed *me* up some, and here we was all goin to the Pink Cat Club together not five minutes after Slim had sat so glum and sad. Grandpa, life ain't happy, and then it's happy, and goes on like that till you die, and you don't know why, and can't ask nobody but God, and He don't say nothin, do He? Grandpa, Slim and Sheila was so fine that night I *knowed* God was on their side jess then, and I thanked Him. Ain't I right, grandpa, to pray when I feel grateful and glad like I did then? Well, that's what I done.

The man zipped that car, and ever'body was glad, and it started rainin but nobody paid it mind, and we got to the club real early and set *parked* in front of it a minute whilst Slim and the men had theirselves a smoke and talked. We was still in *Harlem* about thirty streets up along the way, and it still looked like jess where we lived. The rain got on the street and made the purtiest manner of red and green lights, jess like a Arabian Nights and made rainbows. It was a fine rainy night for Slim to start workin inside that club in, and for me and Sheila to hear him. Well we shore had fun in that car. Slim took out the horn again and went *"BAWP"* with it to try out the lowliest note and

then tried a run up and down the middle notes,
and finished up with a little high *"BEEP"* and
ever'body laughed. "Ouch my fingers," Slim said.
Those two fellows was fine fellows, Charley and
th'other man, 'case they shore admired Slim and
watched.

"Only thing, Slim," Charley said, "that suit of
yours is a little beat." Slim's suit was his onliest
suit, and it was a old blue coat with the whitebelly
insides showin out under the arms, and there was a
rip in the pants he didn't have time to sew up.
Charley said "I know it's the only suit but this Pink
Cat joint is s'posed to be a *cocktail lounge,* you
know, nobody's satisfied anymore with a regular
old saloon."

"Well," Slim laughed, and didn't care, "less go
play some music."

And we all went in the Pink Cat Club suit or no
suit, on time or early or what-all, you know. Well,
it was early. The boss wasn't there yet. The bandstand wasn't lit up. Folks was drinkin at the bar
and playin the big *jukebox* machine and talkin low.

Slim ran up the bandstand, and clicked on the
light. "Come on Charley, let's have some piano."
Charley allowed it was too early and hung back
shy, but Slim allowed no such thing and dragged
him up there. Charley said the other boys in the
band wasn't here yet but it made no difference to
Slim. The other man that was with us, he was the
drummer, and didn't say nothin, but just sat down

behind Slim and knocked the drum and chewed his gum. Well, when Charley seen this he decided to sit down at the piano and play the music too.

Sheila bought me a Coca-Cola and made me sit down in the corner by myself to watch. She stood up right in front of Slim whilst he played his first number and didn't ever move from there till he was finished, and he played the whole first song to her. He blew in the horn, and moved his poor fingers, and I tell you grandpa he made the purtiest deepdown horn-sound like when you hear a big New York City boat way out in the river at night, or like a train, only he made it sing up and down melodious. He made the sound all trembly and sad, and blew so hard his neck shaked all over and the vein popped in his brow, as he carried along the song in front of the piano, and the other man swisht the drum with the broom brushes soft and breezy. And on they went. Slim never took his eye away from Sheila till the middle of the song, then he remembered me and looked across the room and pointed the horn at me and play extra purty to show me how good he could play even though his hands was hurt and he couldn't work in that old cookie factory. Then he turned the horn back to Sheila and finished the song with his head way down on the mouthpiece and the horn against his shoe, and stood like that bowed.

Well you know, ever'body at that bar clapped, and was excited too, and one man said "You

blowed that one, son," and I could see they liked
Slim better and shut down that *jukebox* by all
means.

Sheila come over and sat with me, and there we
was, right by the window and could see the purty
lights out on the wet street, and see the whole bar
and all the folks in front of us, and the bandstand
perfect. Now Slim beat down his feet real fast and
the drummer man walloped one, and off they went
and jumped. Whoo! Slim jess grabbed that horn
and hoisted it up and blew with all his might and
moved his head from side to side with his jaws
workin hard and fast like workin with his hands
that day. When I seen that I realized how strong
Slim was all over, and made of iron.

Ever'body at the bar jumped when they heard
him.

"Yes, yes, yes, yes," yelled that man at the bar
and grabbed his hat and hung on to it and stepped
up and down in front of ever'body jazzy. He shore
could make his feets go, that gen'l'man. Well, he
was dancin to Slim.

Slim, he was walkin up and down where he was
and jess carryin along that jump-song goin as fast,
well, like that *bus* I was tellin you about earlier. He
was pushin the horn to go ever' old way zippin
here and zoopin there, he then all drawed-out himself on one breath way high up, and threw it way
down *"BAWP"* and back again in the middle, and
the drummer-man looked up from his crashing

sticks and yelled "Go Slim!" jess like that. Charley, he was poundin on the piano with all his fingers spread, *blam*, jess when Slim is catchin his breath, and *blam* again when Slim comes back. Grandpa, Slim had more breath than ten men and could go on all night like that. Wow, I never heard anything like it, and anybody makin some noise and music by himself. Sheila, she jess sat there grinnin at her old Slim and knocked her hands together under the table to the beat of the drum. Well, I done the same thing. I shore wished I could dance right then.

"Go, go, go!" yelled that man with the hat and flipped himself back and pawed at the air with his arms and said "Great-day-in-the-mornin!" jess as loud as a big old fog-horn 'bove the noise. Whee, he was funny.

Well now Slim was startin to sweat because nobody wanted to stop, and he didn't wantsa stop neither and blew right on in that horn till the sweat begun pourin down his face jess like it did over the shovel in the mornin. Oh, he jess watered that bandstand from sweat. He didn't ever run out of anything to play ever'time he crossed from one end of the song to th'other, and had a hunnerd years in him of it. Oh, he was grand. That song lasted twenty minutes and the folks at that bar got out in front of the bandstand and clapped in time for Slim in one great big jumpin gang. I could jess see Slim over their heads with his face all black and wet and like he was cryin and laughin all at the same time, only his eyes was closed and he didn't see them but jess plain knew they was there. He was holdin, and pushin that horn in front of him like it was his *life* he was rasslin with, and jess as solemn about it, and unhappy. And ever' now and then he made it laugh too, and ever'body laughed along with it. Oh, he talked and talked with that thing and told his story all over again, to me, to Sheila and ever'body. He jess had it in his heart what ever'body wanted in *their* hearts and they listened to him for some of it. That crowd rocked under him, it was like the waves and he looked like a man makin a storm in that ocean with his horn. One time he let out a big horselaugh with his horn, and hung on to it when ever'body yelled to hear more, and made all kinds of designs with it till it didn't sound like a horselaugh no more but a mule's *heehaw*. Well, they axed him to hold that but he moved on to a high, long drawed-out whistle that sounded like a dog whistle and pierced into my ears, but after awhile it didn't pierce no more but jess was there like ever'thing was made dizzy like Slim felt from holdin that long note. It made you sympathize before he jumped on down back to reg'lar notes and made ever'body jump and laugh again.

A bunch of new folks come in and Slim seen them and decided to end the song there.

It wasn't time to play yet anyhow. He wiped

himself with a towel from the kitchen and we all sat down together in the corner, with Charley and the drummer-man. A man come over from the bar and axed Slim if he ever played with a big band. "Ain't I seen you with Lionel Hampton or Cootie Williams or somebody?" Slim said no, and the man said: "You ought to be with a big band and start makin yourself some money. You don't want to play for peanuts in a place like this all your life, with a taped-up horn. Go down see an agent."

"Agent?" Slim said. "Is that who you see to work with a band?" Slim was s'prised and didn't know any of these things.

Another man come by, and laughed, and shook Slim's hand, and walked back to the bar, jess like that without talkin.

This was how they liked Slim, and what a real fine musician he was.

Well, here come the boss walkin in at nine o'clock, and the rest of the band is with him, includin the leader, who was Charley's older brother, and they all get ready to go on the bandstand. But that big sharped-up boss man seen Slim's tear under his coat and said, "Haven't you got a better suit than that? No? Can't you borrow one from one of these boys?" Ever'body looked at ever'body else, and talked about it, and come to figure there wasn't but one suit they could loan him, only it was down in Baltimore. Well, Baltimore is a long ways off, and the boss had to admit it when he thought about it, but he jess didn't seem to like the idea of Slim in that poor awful suit. He hedged and hawed about it, and began shakin his head after awhile, and I began to see Slim's chance to make five dollars was all ready to go wrong. Slim seen that, and argued with the boss. He said "It don't make no difference, nobody'll see me, looky here I'll hold my arms down" and showed him.

"Well," said that boss, "I know but I'm havin a big holiday crowd tonight and it'll be pretty *toney* as it gets in the later hours, and it just wouldn't look good, don't you see. It's just not, ah, hem, the *thing*." And if you ask me, grandpa, I'd say he wanted to save that five dollars anyhow. One of the boys in the band was sick and Slim was only takin his place, and the boss figured he didn't need nothin or nobody, and didn't.

So out we went, Slim, Sheila and me, to go home, and walked it this time, in the rain. And you know the first thing Slim said?:—"I didn't really get goin on that horn tonight," and that was what he was worried about. Sheila didn't say nothin, but jess held Slim's arm and marched along with him, and enjoyed the walk, and seemed gay.

Well, Slim asked her what she was so gay about, and she told him. You know how poor they was, and the money worries they had that very day, and the rent comin up in a day or two like Slim said. And you know how Slim was always talkin about Californy, and seemed to hint to Sheila about her comin there with him. I didn't tell you, but he come from Californy to marry her before he come to get me, and was out there most of the time since he left North Carolina in his boyhood. Well, Sheila took all that and wrapped it up in one package for Slim, like a Christmas present, and said "Let's use that hundred dollars in my girdle and go to California. I'll tell my mother we have to do it and can't help it. We'll stay at my sister's house in San Francisco to start with. Then we can get jobs, there as well as here I guess. What do you think?"

"Baby," laughed Slim and hugged her, "that's just what I want to do."

And that's how we come to decide to go to Californy, on that day Slim lost two jobs.

11. PACKING FOR CALIFORNY

WE SPENT TWO WHOLE DAYS PACKIN. Sheila's
mother lived right around the corner and come to
visit us three, four times to argue with Sheila about
goin to Californy *cold* like that. Seems Sheila's
family lived in New York so long, with such long
jobs, they didn't believe in traipsin around the
country like that, and once tried to stop Sheila's
sister from goin to Californy, that was Zelda, the
one we was goin to live with out there. But Slim
said, "New York people are always afraid to move
from where they are. Californy is the place to be,
not New York. Didn't you ever hear that song Californy Here I Come, Open Up That Golden Gate?
All that sun, and all that land, and all that fruit,
and cheap wine, and crazy people, it don't scare
you so much when you can't get a job because

then you can always live some way if you even just eat the grapes that fall off the wine trucks on the road. You can't pick no grapes off the ground in *New York,* nor walnuts either."

"Now who's talkin about eatin *grapes* and walnuts?" yelled Sheila's mother. "I'm talkin about a roof over your head." She was a woman of some level sense.

"You don't need one in Californy because it's never cold," said Slim, and laughed in his head gleeful. "Oh, you ain't never seen such nice sunny days when you don't need a *coat* most the year round, and don't have to buy coal to heat your house, or get overshoes or nothin. And you never die of the heat in the summer up north in Frisco and Oakland and thereabouts. I tell you, that's the place to go. Ain't nowhere else to go in the United States and it's the last place on the map—after it, ain't nothin but water and Russia."

"And what's wrong with *New York?*" Sheila's mother snapped up.

"Oh, nothin!" Slim pointed out the window. "Atlantic Ocean is got the Devil for the wind in the wintertime, and the Devil's son carries it down the streets so's a man can freeze to death in a doorway. God brought the sun over Manhattan Island, but the Devil's cousin won't let it in your window unless you get yourself a penthouse a mile high and you don't dass step out of it for a breath of air for fear you'll fall that mile, if you could afford a pent-

house. You can go to work, but probably wind up
havin two hours left to yourself after a eight-hour
day made into twelve hours by subway, bus, elevated, tube, ferry, escalator, and elevator and
waitin in between, it's so *big* and hopeless town.
Ain't nothin wrong with New York, nope. Go
around the corner to see your friend after supper,
see if he's there or ten miles downtown wishin he
could see you. Try to have a ensemble evenin when
your pockets are empty, like any country boy, and
the man'll look for a blackjack in your pants."

That's how *he* talked about things.

"Future of the United States was always goin to
Californy, and always bouncin back from it, and
always will be."

"Well don't come bouncin back on *me* if you go
broke out there," said Sheila's mother and said it
to Sheila.

"We're broke as it is," Sheila said, and that
woman her mother shore didn't like any of it.

Well, I didn't tell you about the money, but
there wasn't enough for all three of us to go by bus.
Sheila was goin to have her first baby before six
months so she had to take sixty dollars of the hunnerd and go by bus and *eat good.* Me and Slim, we
had the forty dollars and some more him and
Sheila still had, and because rent was due in two
days we was movin out, and sendin clothes and
dishes in two big old suitcases and a smaller one,
by railroad, and then me and Slim, with that $48,

was *hitchhikin* to the Coast right away, and eat good too but be *on the bum with our thumbs* and sleep in beds only part of the time, mostly in cars and trucks and parks in the afternoon.

It shore sounded good and fine to me. But I didn't know *then* how far that Californy Coast was.

The last night ever'thing was packed and ready to go in the mornin and we had coffee in the kitchen and house looked so bare Slim seemed most gloomy about it. "Look at this place we've been livin in. We leave it, someone else comes in, and life is jess a dream. Don't it remind you of old cold cruel world to look at it? Those floors and bare walls. Seemed we never lived here, and I never loved you inside of it."

"We'll make ourselves a new home in Californy," said Sheila, gladly.

"What I want is a *permanent* home and spend our lives in one neighborhood, up on a hill till I get old and grandpa."

"We'll see," said Sheila, "and pretty soon Pic'll have a little brother in Californy."

"First we've got to go three thousand and two hundred miles," sighed Slim, and I remembered that later. "Three thousand and two hundred miles," he said, "over a plain, a desert and three mountain chains and any and all the rain that feels like fallin down. Praise the Lord." Well, we went to bed and slept the last night in that house, and sold

the beds in the mornin. "Now we're out in the
cold," Slim said, and he was right. In the afternoon
we left the house dead empty except for a old bottle of milk, and my North Carolina socks too.

Sheila had her suitcase, and me and Slim had
one suitcase with all our things in it. Off we went,
to the bus station, and bought Sheila's ticket and
waited around for her time to go.

By the time her bus was ready we all felt terrible
sad and scared. "There I go into the night," Sheila
said when she saw that bus that said CHICAGO
on it. "I'm goin and I'll never probably come back
again. It's jess like dyin to go to Californy—but
here I come." Grandpa, I ain't forgot that minute.

"It'll be more like livin when you get there,"
Slim laughed, and Sheila said she hoped so. "Don't
let no boys mess with you on that bus," Slim said,
"because you're plumb alone till Pic and me get
there, which I don't know when."

"I'll be waitin for you, Slim," and Sheila begun
cryin. Well, Slim didn't cry but he looked it when
he hugged her. Poor girl—she shore seemed pitiful
that night, and I shore loved her plenty, jess like
Slim said I would on that first night in the woods.
Jess a young mother, and don't know what'll happen to her on the other side of the country, and all
that nighttime alone in front of her till Slim and I
got there. Jess like the Bible said, A fugitive and a

vagabond shalt thou be in the earth, only she was a girl. I reached out and touched her cheek, and told her wait for us in Californy.

"You be extra careful with yourselves hitch-hikin," she said. "Still seems to me Pic is too little for such hard travelin, well, and I don't feel right about it."

But Slim said I'd be safe and sound with him, as much as *he* could be by himself, and if he couldn't make it nobody could. This's how Slim felt, and was sure, and watched over us. So him and Sheila kissed, and then she kissed me so soft and sweet, and in the bus she goes.

"Goodbye Sheila," I said, and waved, and felt more so terrible lonesome and scairt than when she cried, and goodbye, goodbye ever'body else was sayin to ever'body else round the bus, and grandpa that's how sad it is to travel and roam, and try to live and go about things, I reckon till the day you die.

So Sheila went, and was gone, and now me and Slim had to catch up with her hitchhikin over that land.

We walked from the bus station to a big lit-up street called Times Square, and Slim said we was goin out the way we come in, at the Lincoln Tunnel, and hoped that old hole would point us to the West and nowhere else when we shot out of it. "First we'll have our Hot Dog Number One on Times Square," he said.

That's what we done, and grandpa I'll never forget that night of Hot Dog Number One on Times Square, jess about an hour it took us to eat it, before we hit that road.

12. TIMES SQUARE AND THE MYSTERY OF TELEVISION

THERE WAS A WHOLE LOT OF MEN STANDIN on the corner of Eighth Avenue and Forty Second in front of a big gray bank that was closed for the night. In the middle of the road it was all tore up from constructin work, and cars bumped by over the rocky sand along the sidewalk. It was a cold night for spring, felt more like autumn weather, and a whole lot of papers blowed by in the wind and the lights shined ever'whichside and flashed in that wind like so many eyes twinklin. It was jolly, and people had to be a wee bit frisky to keep warm, so they jumped about. Me and Slim bought the hot dogs and spread some mustard on em, and strolled over to the corner to see what was goin on while they cooled a minute.

Lord, there was a couple two, three hunnerd men on one side of the street. Most of them was listenin to the speeches of the Salvation Army. Four Salvations took turns makin speeches, and while one was speakin the other three jess stood there like ever'body else lookin up and down the street to see what else was goin on. Here come a tall white-haired man of ninety years old clompin thu the crowd with a pack on his back, and when he seen ever'body listenin to the speeches he raised his right hand and said *"Go moan for man"* as clear and loud as a foghorn in the wind, and clomped right on by like he hadn't a minute to stop awhile. "Where you goin Pop?" a man said in the crowd, and the old man yelled it back over his head— *"California* my boy"—and he was gone around the corner with that white hair flowin.

"Well," said Slim, "he's not lyin and that's the tunnel he's headed for."

Then here come a loud siren motorcycle, and then another, and a third, all screechin together and escortin the way thu the traffic fo a big black limousine with a spotlight on it. All the men on the corner stooped down to see who was in that car. Me and Slim coulda reached out and touched it and made it a sign, it was so close. The limousine slowed in the sand, and started again, and a man in the crowd yelled "Look out for that Arkansas clay" and some of the men laughed because here it was New York clay and not much of it. Well, wasn't nobody inside the limousine except two, three men with hats on, you know.

Then, grandpa, the word come floatin by in the heaven and I was so scairt, I'd never seen no such thing in all my born days like a word floatin by in the heaven, but Slim said it was jess a old balloon with a electric sign on it nudgin down close to Times Square for ever'body to see. Well, a couple folks looked up and didn't look s'prised, and I *knowed* these New Yorkers was ready and used to ever'thing. It was a purty balloon, and hovered around the longest time, and had to fight with the wind, but tacked and rassled right up there for Times Square. Not so many folks was lookin at it, a shame, bein such a purty balloon like that. Well, my cousins back in Carolina would appreciate it shore a lot. I know I did. It turned its nose into the wind, and wobbled, and jess floated back like a breeze and turned its nose around again and had to buck on back. It was best when it missed and ballooned. I couldn't hear what the poor thing sounded like there was so much fuss below.

A number of things like this was goin on, and those Salvation Army speechers howled right along in the noise and roar. The Lord *this* and the Lord *that* is all they kept sayin, and I don't remember exactly, except about *burning in the fires of repentance* and them talkin to ever'body like they was sinners. Well, maybe ever'body do be sinners but it ain't innerestin on the street corner to hear it challenged, 'case there ain't nobody likely to step up and confess all his sins in front of the police-man that's always teeterin on his heels right there. What's I goin to explain to the police-man about the fire I started in Mr. Otis' cornfield that cost him twenty dollars of feed and nobody ever knowed it was me. Well, no New York man that lives right there is goin to step up and tell how he threw his cigarette away and burned down the hos-pital in his block, and any such thing. Besides of which, why don't the speechers go into detail about *their* own sins they keep repentin and folks could work from there and judge. But it grew in-nerestin when a new man stepped up on the other side of the corner and started a speech of his own. He had a much louder voice and drew a bigger crowd. And it was the shabbiest crowd drew about *him.* He was jess a ordinary lookin man in a black hat, with shiny eyes.

"Ladies and gentlemen of the world, I have come to tell you about the mystery of television. Television is a great big long arm of light that reaches clear into your front parlor, and even in the middle of the night when there ain't no shows going on that light is on, though the studio is dark. Study this light. It will hurt you at first, and bom-bard your eyes with a hundred trillion electronic particles of itself, but after awhile you won't mind it no more. Why?" he yelled way up loud and Slim said "Yes!" The man said, "Because while electric-

ity was light to see by, *this* is the light comes not to
see by, but to *see*—not to read by, but to *read.* This
is the light that you *feel.* It is the first time in the
world that light has been gathered up from the
sources of light and shot through a tube in a way
that it can be watched and studied instead of
blinked at. And it has taken the shape of men and
women who are real flesh and blood at the studio
but come streaming into your parlor in *light* with
all their sounds shot in sidetrack. What does this
mean, ladies and gentlemen?"

Well, nobody knowed that, and waited, and
Slim said "Go, man!" and to hear it.

"It means that man has discovered light and is
fiddling with it for the first time, and has released
concentrated shots of it into everyone's house, and
nobody yet knows what the effect will be on the
mind and soul of people, except that now there is a
general feeling of nervousness among some, and
sore eyes, and twitching of nerves, and a suspicion
that because it has come at the same time as the
A T O M there may be an unholy alliance betwixt
one and the other, and both are bad and injurious
and leading to the end of the world, though some
optimists claim it is the opposite of the atom and
may relax the nerves the atoms undid. Nobody
knows!" he moaned way out loud, and looked at
ever'body frank. Well, ever'body was innerested
and paid no attention to the speeches about *repentance,* and Slim agreed, most amazed.

"And ladies and gentlemen," he said, "it is the old-time Depression traveling salesman that used to put his foot in your door and now has got a leg in your parlor, except he looks so doggone strange in light you just can't believe his transformation. And don't think *he* ain't more nervous than the Depression days jiggling behind all that light and looking out into the unknown America. Yes ladies and gentlemen and I seen a salesman on television last night who put on a mask for fun and yet his eyes looked awfully scared peeking from behind that mask at a million other better-hidden eyes. What does this mean?" he demanded, and ever-'body was ready to kneel to find out, so to speak, and Slim yelled "Go!" and socked his hands together.

"The day shall come when one giant brain shall televize the Second Coming in light and everyone in the world shall see it in their brains by means of a brain-television that Christ Himself shall cause to be switched on in a miracle and no one shall be spared from knowing the Truth, and everyone shall be saved forever, and men and women of the world I warn you, live as best as you can and be hereinafter kind to one another and that is all there is to do now. We all know this." And off he trots jess as calm as you please, and Slim looked after him with the most satisfied and glad look and clapped his hands, so that a whole bunch of others clapped their hands too, and the speecher vanished in glory. Grandpa, it was as strange as that.

Then the Salvation Army man howled out at us "Don't you realize the Lord is coming?" and jess then a loud screechin and crashin come down the street flamin red lights ever'whichway and I ducked, it was the fire engines barrelin to a fire with a whole bunch of firemen hangin on to their hats most solemn and displeased, and goin a hunnerd miles a hour. Whoo! that roused us, and Slim said "Whee!" and ever'body shore looked amazed and innerested then ever'thing got back to normal and people slouched around bored like always.

Well, it was time to go, and Slim said, "We'll come back to Times Square sometime, but now we gotsa go across that night, like the old man with the white hair, and keep goin till we get on the other side of this big, bulgin United States of America and all the raw land on it, before we be safe and sound by the Pacific Sea to set down and thank the Lord. Are you ready Pic?" he said, and I said "Yes," and off we go.

13. THE GHOST OF THE SUSQUEHANNA

It was eight o'clock when we went and stood in front of the Lincoln Tunnel in all that yaller light, and it started mistin jess a little, enough to worry me and Slim even before we was begun on the road. But for the first time since that time, we got a ride inside a minute; seemed like the man at the wheel come around the corner sayin "pleased to meet you" before we could even show our thumbs. He lit up with a smile and throwed open the door. It was a big gigantic yaller truck that said PENSCO on it, with a tractor-cab in front a good twelve feet high, and the biggest tires in the world, and hauled a trailer you couldn't see over of without backin up across the street. A mighty gigantic thing, that Slim had to throw me up to get in, and the man cotch me like a football. When I sat up

218

there it felt like bein in a tree, it was so grand and
high. Slim jumped after, and hauled in that suitcase that had all our clothes, and here we go.

"Going someplace with your kid brother?" the
driver said. "It don't do for him to get caught in
the rain," and with that he kicked down, and
grabbed two clutches, and socked ever'thing
around and pumped his feet like an organ-player,
and boom! that big truck started to roll and growl,
and bowled down into the tunnel like a mountain.
It was a white man drivin it. His name was Nori-
dews. And he made that tunnel shake and rever-
berate from there to New Jersey.

Not only that he didn't say another word till we
got to Pennsylvania hours later, and all Slim and
me had to do was sit and enjoy the way he throwed
that gigantic machine down the highway. He was
ever so much stronger than a poor *bus,* and that is
a heap of strength. People in the other cars seemed
to quake and wobble when we come by spit-boom
eatin up ever'thing in sight. Only time he stopped
was on a hill, and only stopped *passin* people then,
didn't stop rollin at all. He had the mightiest
brakes in the world to stop that trailer bumpin us
down the back at ever' red light, and had to kick
for his life on the brakes they handled such powerful stops and was so supple. Then the trailer
bucked to a stop, like a mule, and edged along like
it couldn't wait too long at no red light, and the

driver told it to hold fast but it edged along no lesser. "She's got to go," he said.

Well, the mist was rainin in New Jersey, and grandpa, the first thing Slim and I seen was that old white man with the silver hair flowin around his head, walkin along in the highway in all that yaller light with the rain blowin over him like the smoke. Oh, he looked pitiful and grand all at the same time for an old man. Slim said, "He got a poor short ride from New York." We looked at him when we boomed by, and seen his face stuck out in the rain and him deep in thought of somethin like it never rained and like he wasn't anywhere but in his room, you know. "What's he goin to do?" Slim said, and "Oh that wonderful gentleman he puts me in the mind of Jesus, trackin along like that in this dismal world. I bet he don't pay no taxes, neither, and his toothbrush was lost in Hoover's Army. Ah," he said, "ever'body's bound to make it at the same time if *he* ever makes it." The old man had the bluest eyes, I seen that when we rolled by. Seen him later, tell you when some day.

We rolled through all the crowded streets of New Jersey, and got on the road, and come to a sign that said "South" with an arrow pointin flat to the left, and "West" with an arrow pointin straight down, and stayed right on the straight arrow down into the West. It got dark, and countrylike, and pretty soon there was hills.

It took some hours to get to Pennsylvania where the man was drivin to, and about five to get to Harrisburg, Pennsylvania, where he lived. I slept some of the way. It kept right on rainin. Inside the cab was warm and comfortable, and a good start it was for me and Slim. He said he wasn't far behind Sheila after all.

At Harrisburg at midnight the man said he could save time by droppin us off outside town at a junction and pointed to it when we passed, and it was a lonely rainy junction that made me gulp it was so dark, but he said he would take us in anyhow to make sure we connected right for Pittsburgh and points west, and added he knowed another short cut downtown. That was good for us, that short cut. Harrisburg was all lit up in halos in the rain and looked quiet and gloomy. There was big gray bridges, and the Susquehanna river below them, and the main street in town where ever'body was waitin for buses at midnight.

Me and Slim jumped out of the tractor-cab at the red light, and the man repeated his instructions over whilst Slim thanked him gladly, and then back we was on foot, goin slant across town for the other highway with hopes on high. "That was a good ride," Slim said, "and I wouldn't of got one like it alone. Ever'body'll sympathize with you bein so little and we'll make time to the Coast. Pic, you're my goodluck chile. Come along with me you old daddyo."

The houses in Harrisburg is extremely old, and come from the time of George Washington, Slim said. They's all old brick in one part of town, and have crooked chimbleys and ancient shapes but look all neat. Slim said the town was so old because it was on a great old river. "Ain't you ever heard of the Susquehanna, and Daniel Boone and Benjamin Franklin and the French and Italian wars? In those times ever'body was here, and come from New York where we was, with pushcarts and oxes over the hills that truck groaned on, in rain and high weather, and suffered and died jess to reach it here. It was the beginnin of the big long push to California and now you remember how long it took us to get here by truck then figure it by ox, and *then* tell me about it when we get to San Francisco—about the ox. I'll ask you about it when we go over the sink in Nevady. In Nevady they's a sink that took down a *whole ocean* and's been dry ever since, and takes a month to measure the edges of it. Ain't nobody wash their teeth over that sink. You ain't seen nothin yet, boy."

Well, we was still in Susquehanna and hungry enough to be in Nevady, so Slim said we'd have Hot Dog Number Two and Hot Dog Number Three and maybe Four. We went to a diner and ate them, and had a side dish of beans with katchup, and coffee both of us. Slim said I had to learn to drink coffee to keep warm on the road. He counted his money, said we had $46.80 left, and dug down in the suitcase to put on more clothes in case it rained bigger. He said he hoped we got a ride soon so's I could sleep, and wished I could wake up in Pittsburgh and then we'd move right on 'stead of sleepin. "Up ahead the sun is shinin in Illinois and Missouri, I *know* it," he said.

By and by we hit the night again, and Slim brought along two packs of cigarettes that left us $46.40, and we walked to the outskirts of town. Folks looked at us curious and wondered what we was doin. Well, that's life. *A man's got to live and get there,* Slim always said about that. "Life is a sneeze, life is a breeze," he said. Along come a car with a man goin home from work and Slim didn't care, he threw out his thumb and whistled 'most shrill through his teeth, and when he seen the man wouldn't stop, why he stuck his leg and pulled up the pants and said "Have pity on a poor young girl of the road." Tickled me the way he fooled around ever'where he went.

It was cold, and it *was* raw, but we felt real fine jess like we was home. Ever' now and then I got to worryin about findin a bed and home in Californy, and worried about Sheila, and worried about gettin tireder than I was, and damper, in a darker place than this, but Slim made me forget it the way he went along. "It's the only way to live," Slim said, "jess don't die. Whoopee, sometimes I feel like dyin but now I wantsa wait the *longest* time. Bein that you bring it in some more, Lord, I ain't

afraid of a few cold toes so long's my whole foot
don't crack. Lord, you didn't give me any money
but you gave me the right to *complain.* Whoo!
Complain so long on the left hand, the other
hand'll fall off. Well, I've got my baby, I'll hold on
jess a while longer, and see what Californy looks
like now, and look around inside myself, and bet. I
can't do no more than *kick,* Lord, kick this way,
kick that way, and then I kick it proper. Look out
for you boy, Lord." Slim was always talkin to God
like that. We got to know each other fine and could
talk to ourselves anytime, the other one only listened. I'd say "Tick, tack, toe!" countin my foot-
steps and Slim would say "There you go!" jess as
absent-minded and thinkin about somethin else. It
was the grandest fun, and good.

Someday grandpa I'll make a whole lot of
money for you and me, but I'll enjoy it like Slim
enjoyed it *without* no money, and make sure to be
a happy man.

We crossed over the town, and pretty soon there
we was on the highway and there was the Susquehanna River runnin right with us, most solemn and
black and not makin a sound for miles.

And here come a man with a little tiny suitcase
hurryin along most jaunty from the shore, and
seen us, and waved, and said "Walk a little faster if
you want to keep up with me, for I'm goin to
CANADY and I don't aim to waste time." Well,
he wasn't even caught up with us and talked like

that, but soon enough he passed us. "Can't lag, son, can't lag," he said, and was lookin back. Me and Slim hurried on after him quick.

"Where you headed?" Slim said, and the man— he was jess a little old man, white, and poor—said "Why, I'm gonna get me a HIBALL up the river here soon's I cross the bridge. Member of the Veterans of Foreign Wars and the American Legion. Red Cross in this town wouldn't give me a dime. Tried to sleep in the railyards last night and they put a spotlight on me. Told them 'You'll never see me in *this* town again,' walked away. Had a good breakfast last week, Martinsburg, West Virginia, pancakes, syrup, ham, toast, two glasses milk and a haif, and a Mars candy bar. Always like to load up for the winter like a squirrel. Had grits and brains in Hippensburg two weeks now, and wasn't hungry for three days."

"You mean Harrisburg?"

"Hippensburg, son, Hippensburg, Pennsylvania. I've got to meet my pardner in Canady by month's end so I can go into a uranium deal. Know upstate New York!" he said wavin his fist most determined. He was a funny old man, was short and thin, all weazled up his face that had such a long horny nose, and looked so shrunk and wan under his hat I wouldn't recognize if I seen him again. "Walk fast," he yelled to usn's behind, "knew a boy three years ago on this road jess the same as

you. Lazy! Slow! Don't lag!" We followed him
and had to hustle some.

We walked about two mile.

"Where we goin?" Slim said.

"Know what I had me in Harrisburg last night?
One fine meal I tell you, in any diner in the world.
Had candied pig's feet, yams, with peas, peanut
butter sandwich and two cups tea and Jello with
fruits in it. Old Veteran of Foreign Wars cook behind the counter. On the twelfth of this month had
me a cold shower followed by hot, in the Cameo
Hotel, won't tell you where, desk clerk was Jim,
Veteran of Foreign Wars, I caught a cold and
sneezed myself all over."

"You sure keep movin along, Pop," said Slim.

"Old silver-haired man with a pack an hour ago
couldn't even keep up with me. All set for Canady,
I am. Got things in this bag. Got a nice new necktie, too." His bag was a poor little tore-up piece of
cardboard and was held together by a big belt tied
around it. He kept fiddlin at the belt. "Wait a sec-
ont while I take out that tie," he said, and we all
stopped in front of a empty gas station and he
kneeled down to undo the belt.

I sat down and caught back the rest in my legs,
and watched. That man was so funny, that was
why Slim was followin him and talkin to him so.
Slim jess went along trailin what innerested him,
you know, and couldn't say no to any old man like
that.

"Now where can that tie be?" said the old man, and fiddle-faddled around in his busted satchel the longest time, and scratched his haid. "Now don't tell me I left it in Martinsburg. I packed two dozen cough drops that morning and remember the tie was stuck up alongside. No it wasn't Martinsburg at all, at all, at all, now where was it? Harrisburg? Ah shoot, this old tie will do till I get to Ogdensburg, New York State," and off we went again walkin. He didn't have no such a tie.

Grandpa don't believe it if you will, but we walked SIX more miles along that river with that old man, and somethin was supposed to be around the bend ever' time, but there never was anything. I never walked so much and minded it so little, he talked so crazy. "I have all my papers," he kept sayin, and told us what he done in ever' town for the past month to eat, how he showed his cridentials at places, and what the meal was, and how much sugar he put in his coffee and crackers in his soup. It made me and Slim hungry to hear him. He's so small, and loved food so large. And walked, and walked.

Well, that somethin never showed up and we had walked clear into the wilderness where the road lit in only the longest spaces.

Slim stopped cold, and said "Say, you must be . . ." but didn't wanta say "crazy" and just said "You must be . . . Pop, me and my brother better turn back."

"Back? No back about this part of the country. Heh heh. I just misjudged you boys like I misjudged that young man three years ago, that's all I done. I'm ready to go on if you ain't."

"Well, we can't walk all night," Slim said.

"Go ahead, give up, I'm all set to walk to Canady and straight on through New York City if that's how the chips fall."

"New York City?" Slim yelled. "Did I hear you say? Ain't this the road west to Pittsburgh?"

Slim stopped, but the man hurried right along. "Say, did you hear me?" Slim yelled. That old man heard him all right but didn't care. "Keep walking," I say, "maybe I'll be in Canady, maybe I won't. Can't wait around all night." And he kept talkin, and walkin, till all we could see was his shadow fadin in the dark and gone like a ghost.

"Well," Slim said, "it *was* a ghost." And he worried himself to death standin there with me in those fearful river woods, at midnight, tryin to figure where we was and how we got lost. All I could hear now was the pat of rain on a million leaves, and the chug-chug across the river, and my own heart beatin in all that open air. Lord, it's somethin.

"Why'd I go follow that crazy man!" Slim said, and seemed lonesome, and looked for me, and reached some. "Pic, you there?"

"Slim, I'm scairt," I said.

"Well don't be scairt, we'll walk back to town

and get back to those lights and folks can see us. Whoo!"

"Slim, who was that man?" I asked him, and he said, "Shoo, that was some kinda ghost of the river, he's been lookin for Canady in Virginia, West Virginia, West Pennsylvania, North New York, New York City, East Arthuritis and South Pottzawattomy for the last eighty years as far as I can figure, and on foot, too. He'll never find the Canady and he'll never get to Canady because he's goin the wrong way all the time."

So grandpa the next three cars swished by, and the fourth one stopped for us, and we ran for it. Was big solemn white man in a beach-wagon truck. "Yes," he said, "this is the road west to Pittsburgh but you better go back to town for a ride."

"That old man is goin to walk west all night, and he wants to get to the North to Canady," said Slim, and it was the God-awfullest truth, and we was talkin about that Ghost of the Susquehanna for the next three months I tell you when we got to Sheila in San Francisco.

14. HOW WE FINALLY GOT TO CALIFORNY

I'M GOIN TELL YOU IT WAS A LONG TRIP, grandpa.
That man rode us back to Harrisburg in the rain.
He told us how to take a left and then a right and
then left and then right and go down to a lunch
wagon where he said they made very good sweet
yams and pigs' feet and also seven-inch-long hot
dogs with Picadilly Circus on it. Me and Slim went
in there and sat down in the eatin part of the res-
trant, th'other side was a spittoon place with a big
bunch of men argufyin about how they was Jindians.

"Don't tell me that, you're no Indian!"

"Oh I ain't, ain't I?—I'm a Pottzawattomy from
Canady and my mother was pure-bred Cherokee."

"If you're a Pottzawattomy from Canady and

230

your mother was pure-bredded Cherokee I'm
James Roosevelt Turner."

"Well turn around, son, and I'll give you the
biggest whompin you ever got." And then there
was the sound of glasses breakin, and fights, and
hollerin, and women yowlin, and this woman came
over to the table where me and Slim was eatin and
sat down with us with a nice smile and said "May I
join you?" just as a big flock of police-men came in
out of a squad car. The woman, girl actelly, said to
Slim:

"May I sit?"

And she smiled but Slim he was afeared of the
police-men and never smiled back at her smile, besides Slim is married to Sheila, but the woman sat
there actin as though she was at the same table
with us and no one of the police-men offered up to
bother her. Slim didn't say no, and he didn't say
yes. The police-men took away the skeedaddlin
Jindians and ever'thing was peaceful again.

Me and Slim ate up all our money on candy
yams and pigs' knucklets feets and seven-inch-long
hot dogs and Slim didn't pay no intention which-
however to the woman. It was a barnyard. But you
know, grandpa, a whole lot of black men have Jin-
dian blood, as I discovered up when I saw all those
Jindians in Nebraskar, Ioway and Nevady, not to
mention Oakland.

But now we were pretty well filled up with food-supper and ready to roam on in the rainin, only now it was slower now, pizzlin, and Slim said:

"Now next step is to get to Pittsburgh down this Route 22."

It was early mornin sunrisin and an au-to went by and squished a blue-color bird under the rollin wheel.

It made me sickish to hear the squeak of it. I wished there was a better place. I felt missilated. A plumber gave us a ride to Huntingdon, then a light-bulb man gave us a ride to Holidaysburg, then a man called Biddy Blair gave us a ride to Blairsville, then we wound up in Corapolis with a countryfolk truck driver whose son had jess had a hernia belly. It was awful all them stories you heard. But I had a feelin in my chest that ever-'body was doin their best, I guess.

Now it was about seben o'clock in the mornin and Slim bought some Sin-Sins to put sugar in our mouth. He was rare worried he'd never get to Sheila. He didn't not ever tell me how long it was to Oakland for fear I'd get scairt. I told him I didn't know there was so many white people in the world, comin as I done from North Carolina coun-tryfolks.

He said: "Yep."

Then he said: "I wonder if Mr. Otis sent out the cops after me for kidnapin you. Well, he won't find us now. Here's stoppin a car with two men in it."

They was goin eighty miles a hour or somethin

like that but they stopped, squeak. We got in the back. They said:

"Where you goin?—Shoot, we Montana-bound, you got money?"

Slim said "Not much so."

So they said "We'll drop you off at Pittsburgh." It was rainin, grandpa, when we got to Pittsburgh. Me and Slim went inta the railroad station, to get out of the rainin. Two men in blue choo-choo master suits told us to get out. So we pulled up our collars and draddled on down the street, we saw a church, with a cross on top on it. Slim said:

"Let's go in there and dry up some. Don't reckon they'll throw us out of there."

It was chilly-like but there was a runnin heat comin from the furnace in the bottom down-be-lows, and a man upstairs was playin the big organ piano, Slim said it was the Have-a-Maria, and then a fellow come by with a lighted stick and went rush-up lightin candles at the front part, "The Halter," said Slim (said it laughin), and outside it was rainin cats and dogs.

Grandpa, when I heared that music I shushed Slim, and I said:

"Can I sing?"

"Slim wants to know if you know the tune?" said Slim.

"Well I'll jess hum."

Slim said: "Here comes the big man in the black coat."

By this time I was already hummin.

The big man in the black coat said "You have a beautiful voice, what's your name?"

"Pictorial Review Jackson of North Carolina."

"And who's he?"

"My brother John Jackson."

The priest axed "Do you know how to dust pews?"

Slim says "I just worked in a cookie factory and I'd rather dust pews."

"Do you know how to mop floors in the basement? Two Army cots beside the furnace, hundred dollars a month, fifty each, free food, no rent."

Slim says "Tsa deal, we are goin all the way to Californy to join up with my wife."

"What's your wife's name?"

"Sheila Jackson, born Joyner, North Carolina."

"I am Father John McGillicuddy."

Slim sez "Ain't you the guy that managed the Philadelphia Phillies?"

"No, that was Cornelius McGillicuddy, some distant cousin . . . Philadelphia Athletics . . . I am Father John McGillicuddy, Society of Jesus, Jesuit Order. Now little Jackson Picture you want to go up sing in the choir? What's your favorite tune?"

Grandpa I told him *Our Father Which Art in Heaven,* coulda made Lulu cry to hear me sing like that in her porch.

So Father McGillicuddy took me up to the attic

LOFT, and sat me by the man with his hands on the keys of the ORGAN. Grandpa, I even whistled and I wished I had my harmonica, and the priest man sang up and said I sung up like an angel.

By the by, Slim was present down at the cellar moppin up the floor, he said he sure wisht he had his horn, but said he found a horn in his little brother's voice.

So we told Father McGillicuddy soon's we pick up one hunnerd dollars pay we would fetch for Oakland on the Greyhound Bus, but Father McGillicuddy said it was comin up close to Sunday mornin, as it was Adventist or adventurous night now, and Saturday too, and wanted me to sing before the intire congregation the Lord's Prayer, which I done, up in the LOFT, like best I could. Father McGillicuddy was s'tickled he was sunrise all over. Them Irish mans is so tickled they's pink as a shoat all over, but I feasable say they got troubles of their own, so we had our hunnerd dollars and took the road bus with the picture of the blue hound dog on the side of it, Greyhound it's called, and we peewetted across Ohia and clear inta Nebraskar, Slim was asleep in the back seat all alone stretched out legs all over, and I was sittin in a reg'lar seat near-up with a ninety-year-old white man, and when we come to a stop just before Kearney, Nebraskar, the old man said to me:

"I gotta go to the toilet."

So I led him out of the bus holdin his hand, 'case

he was about to fall in the snow, and ask the gas
man where was the men's room. Finished, I took
the old man back in the bus, and the bus driver
yelled out:

"Somebody's drinkin around here!"

And the bus driver was wearin black gloves.
Two men was in the front seat next to him holdin
hands together.

Slim was still snorin on the back-seat bed. Then
he got up said to me:

"Hi, baby."

First thing you know, no more snow. Heard another old man behind me say "I'm goin back to
Oroville and bank my dust."

We then was now in the Sacramenty Valley,
grandpa, and quick we saw Sheila's ropelines with
wash on hooks of wood hung dryin, flappety-flap.

Slim, he put his two hands on his back, limpied
around the yard, and said, "I got Arthur-itis, Bus-
itis, Road-itis, Pic-itis and ever' other It-is in the
world."

And Sheila run up, kissed him hungarianly, and
we went in eat the steak she saved up for us, with
mashy potatoes, pole beans, and cherry banana
spoon ice cream split.

ABOUT THE AUTHOR

JACK KEROUAC was born in 1922 in Lowell, Massachusetts, and died in 1969 in St. Petersburg, Florida. He grew up in Lowell, and later attended Columbia in New York. Leaving school, he sailed with the merchant marine to various Atlantic and Mediterranean ports, and roamed over much of the United States. His first book, *The Town and the City*, was published in 1950. Unable to find a publisher for *On the Road*, he spent the next six years "writing whatever came into my head, hopping freights, hitchhiking, and working as a railroad brakeman, deckhand and scullion on merchant ships, government fire lookout, and hundreds of assorted jobs." *On the Road* was finally published in 1957 and brought him immediate fame. His other books were published in rapid succession and translated into eighteen languages. He is right-fully considered as the authentic voice of the "beat generation" in American literature. His other books include *The Subterraneans, Visions of Neal, Doctor Sax, Lonesome Traveler, The Dharma Bums, Mexico City Blues, Visions of Gerard, Desolation Angels*, and *Satori in Paris. Pic* is his last novel.